THE MARDUK LETTERS

THE MARDUK LETTERS

*Diabolically Eliminating Level 5
and Servant Leaders*

By
Wilbur Reid

RESOURCE *Publications* · Eugene, Oregon

Resource Publications
An Imprint of Wipf and Stock Publishers
199 W. 8th Ave., Suite 3
Eugene, OR 97401

www.wipfandstock.com

PAPERBACK ISBN: 978-1-7252-9046-4
HARDCOVER ISBN: 978-1-7252-9047-1
EBOOK ISBN: 978-1-7252-9048-8

JULY 29, 2022 10:41 AM

Contents

SECTION 2   THE MODEL

Section 1

The Letters

Introduction

THE WAR BETWEEN GOOD AND evil has raged since the beginning of time, and the tip of the spear has been the battle for the hearts and minds of the leaders who influence others. Marduk is the undersecretary of hell who oversees the demon tempters assigned to humans with leadership potential. He is best known for his battle with the Enemy and his prophet Daniel for the leadership influence of Nebuchadnezzar II of Babylon in the seventh century BC.

Marduk was worshipped as a god in the Babylonian empire, and in Nebuchadnezzar's inaugural address he prayed: "O merciful Marduk, may the house that I have built endure forever, may I be satiated with its splendor, attain old age therein, with abundant offspring, and receive therein tribute of the kings of all regions, from all mankind."[1] Marduk heard the prayer and Nebuchadnezzar became the most powerful king in the world.

The pride of Nebuchadnezzar was challenged by four young men who were taken as captives from the land of Judah, as told in the Biblical book of Daniel. When Nebuchadnezzar had a troubling dream, Daniel told the king what he dreamed and interpreted the dream. Being humbled by the miracle, "King Nebuchadnezzar fell prostrate before Daniel and paid him honor and ordered that an offering and incense be presented to him. The king said to Daniel, "Surely your God is the God of gods and the Lord of kings and a revealer of mysteries, for you were able to reveal this mystery

---

1. Mark, "Nebuchadnezzar II."

(Daniel 2:46-47)."[2] However, Marduk was able to restore the king's pride and authoritarian leadership style.

Sixteen years later, Nebuchadnezzar's hubris was evident in the construction of an enormous image of gold and the requirement that everyone bow and worship the image. When Daniel's three friends, Shadrach, Meshach, and Abednego, refused to bow, they were thrown into the fiery furnace. When they emerged unscathed, Nebuchadnezzar again was humbled, saying "Praise be to the God of Shadrach, Meshach, and Abednego, who has sent his angel and rescued his servants! They trusted in him and defied the king's command and were willing to give up their lives rather than serve or worship any god except their own God. Therefore, I decree that the people of any nation or language who say anything against the God of Shadrach, Meshach and Abednego be cut into pieces and their houses be turned into piles of rubble, for no other god can save in this way (Daniel 3:28-29)." Once again, Marduk roused Nebuchadnezzar from this humble position and masterfully manipulated Nebuchadnezzar to a state of arrogance.

The final battle for Nebuchadnezzar's powerful influence centered around a dream that Daniel interpreted predicting that the king would lose his mind and live among animals for seven years before being restored to his thrown. When this prophecy was fulfilled, Nebuchadnezzar acknowledged his weakness, and his last recorded words were that God is able to humble those who walk in pride.

In this current role of undersecretary of hell, Marduk's mentor proteges are recent graduates of the Tempters Training College (TTC). Among the new proteges is his half-witted nephew Slugtoad, who finished first in his graduating class (which would be last in human rankings). Marduk uses handwritten letters to coach and mentor the proteges, which he learned from his peer Screwtape.

Due to the heavy workload of the department, Marduk assigned two patients for each of the young tempters. Slugtoad was

---

2. *The Holy Bible: New International Version, Containing the Old Testament and the New Testament.*

assigned two American college students who are nearing graduation and preparing to enter the "real world." Marduk referred to
the two patients simply as "the man" and "the woman."

Marduk advised Slugtoad to guide the patients away from
effective leadership by discouraging the use of the characteristics
of servant and Level 5 leadership. Each of these two leadership
types is comprised of ten characteristics such as personal humility, indomitable will, and a servant attitude. These characteristics
are showcased in the letters from Marduk. The letters progress
throughout the lives of the patients as they mature from college
students to leaders of many people. Marduk targets the challenges
the patients face in their corporate careers, in their families, and
within the church that they serve. Inexplicably, Slugtoad lost the
letters sent from his uncle. They have been found on Earth and are
published here for your consideration.

We learned from the first set of letters from Screwtape to
Wormwood that the devil is a liar, and that the perspective of hell
is opposite that of heaven. For demons, Satan is Our Father Below,
while God is the Enemy. The goal of every demon is to be demoted
through the lowerarchy of hell.[3]

---

3. Lewis, *The Screwtape Letters.*

1

The Charge

MY DEAR SLUGTOAD,
I noticed at the graduation ceremony of the TTC yesterday that you and your colleagues seemed quite pleased with yourselves and your collegiate accomplishments. However, now it is time to enter the real world and engage in battle with the Enemy. You are fortunate to have been placed on my team because we have the delicious task of tempting leaders of the Enemy's team.

You have no doubt seen in your formative years and academic studies that our battle with the Enemy has progressed as Our Father Below planned. Our past efforts of sowing discord and disunity among Christians has successfully resulted in the horrid evil of numerous sectarian divisions. In recent years, our strategy has been to separate Christians from the broader culture, so they appear to be intolerant and unloving. This has been difficult work for our tempters because the scriptures of the Enemy are full of admonitions to love everyone regardless of differences. However, great progress has been made, and the favorability of Christians and their influence on culture has been steadily declining since I was in your position. Despite the progress, Our Father Below is disturbed by a growing movement within young Christians that is characterized by humility, service, and zeal. If these ideas continue to grow, much of our recent progress is threatened to be undone. If the humans become united and useful to their fellow man, there is a great risk that many in society will turn to the Enemy, and delicious souls will be lost to us.

Since our newly formed team is not yet fully staffed, I am assigning two patients to you. Fortunately for you, at this time they are college students, and neither the man nor the woman have realized they have the potential to exert significant influence. Use this naivete and lack of self-confidence to your advantage. Your assignment is to render them useless as Christian leaders.

My friend Screwtape often reminds me that the safest road to hell is the gradual one. It is imperative that you tempt your patients with small incremental steps without sudden turnings. Inexperienced tempters often make the mistake of attempting to get their patient involved with a significant sexual or financial sin. While gratifying in the short term, it does not produce the most meaningful long-term results because the patient could repent and learn from mistakes and could be even more effective later in life. Their lives are marathons, not sprints. Be patient.

My secretary Toadpipe will forward the dossier on your new patients. Familiarize yourself with every aspect of their lives, including the critical components of their spiritual lives and relationships.

Your affectionate uncle
MARDUK

2

A Team Player and Collaborator

M Y DEAR SLUGTOAD,
Your letter betrays some unfounded cockiness after reading the dossier on your patients. I am glad to see you are not letting your education get in the way of your ignorance.

While it is true that the man is a naïve college student who panics at the thought of speaking in public, there is something within him that is difficult for us to identify currently. Likewise, while the woman is lacking in self-confidence and does not seem to be a threat, she is far more powerful than she knows. You must maintain a healthy respect for their potential and grasp the characteristics that could be utilized to make them effective leaders. Your work will begin with fundamentals that are foundational to becoming an effective leader.

You mentioned in your letter that the man is thinking about trying to join the university basketball team. While participation in sports seems harmless, becoming a part of a team provides several disadvantages to your cause, and you must strongly discourage his participation. The first issue is his development as a person. He will build self-confidence, communication skills, discipline, and time management. Part of this growth will be getting to know people of other racial and socio-economic backgrounds that he might not otherwise become friends with. If he becomes brothers in battle with other types of people, it will be more difficult for you later to suggest stereotypes to demonize people who do not look like him or believe what he believes. Secondly, leadership skills will be developed as he establishes relationships with positive mentors and grows into leadership roles on the team. These skills will include how to inspire and motivate others and how to take decisive action. Finally, you must not allow him to be on a team because he will learn to subjugate his personal desires for the good of the team. This humility and willingness to place others before self is foundational to becoming an effective leader.

The woman is perhaps a greater risk currently. In previous generations we were able to persuade young women that sports were only for boys, which crippled leadership development for half of the humans. However, that argument has been rendered ineffective as an alarming number of girls are joining team sports and other team activities. Your patient has gained the reputation among her university volleyball teammates as an unselfish team player, and they are beginning to see her as a leader. Some are even mentioning that she would be a good captain for next year's team. Nothing will build her confidence faster than if she begins to see herself as a leader, and if the coach validates that confidence by installing her as captain. Therefore, you must convince her that individual pursuits, such as studying to achieve higher grades, are more important and that her participation on the team is a distraction to these worthier goals. You must persuade her to withdraw her passion and dedication to the team.

Perhaps the reasoning behind the correlation behind being a team player and becoming a great leader is alluding you. As your patients mature, they will become a part of multiple teams including a work team, a family, and a church (hell forbid!). If they have a mindset of being a team player who willingly subdues their ego for the good of the team, others will want to follow them, and potential rivals will work with them instead of fighting against them for power within the organization. The team will be more successful, and promotion opportunities will more readily open doors for increased leadership and influence. Collaboration with others is thinking together as a unit and it is powerful, and collaboration begins by working together as a team.

As the patients attain higher levels of influence and higher levels of position within the organization, team players focus on the development of other leaders around them. Our goal is to isolate leaders so that when they leave the organization, it falls apart because there was no leadership development for succession planning. The worst-case scenario is that the leader has mentored and grown leaders around him so that in his absence another leader can quickly step in and fill the void. In sports, everyone on the team is trained to step into the game at a moment's notice if needed. If there is an injury, the replacement is expected to know the position and responsibilities so that there is a minimal decline in the team's performance. Likewise, in leadership, a team player is prepared to do whatever it takes to make the team successful.

Your affectionate uncle
MARDUK

3

Values and Shows Genuine
Interest in All People

M Y DEAR SLUGTOAD,
I am disappointed to hear of your utter lack of
success regarding the involvement of your patients
in teams. You have miles to go before you reach mediocre. You
seemed to feel no embarrassment in informing me that not only
was the woman named captain of her volleyball team, but the man
became a walk-on to the basketball team. Are all the new graduates
of TTC worthless, or are you the exception? I will chalk this up to
your inexperience and move on to address your current situation.

In addition to the leadership development experience on
teams, another reason that you should have persuaded your patients away from teams is the valuation of all teammates. Their
teammates become brothers or sisters with whom they spend a
lot of time and go into battle with. Lifelong bonds are created.
This becomes a particularly significant problem for us when those
teammates are of different races, beliefs, and backgrounds because
racism and other "isms" are difficult to foment when one has
friends of other groups. One of our goals in thwarting Christian
leadership is to divide people into groups so that there is animosity
and even hatred between the groups. That leaves a leader's effectiveness limited to just their small group. Our Father Below has

been ruthlessly effective in dividing Christians over the centuries, which eases our task of stirring up animosity for people who are different. In America, however, the Christians have been making progress as they realize they are the minority and unite against us as a greater common enemy. The denominations are becoming less sectarian and more ecumenical. We are losing ground on race relations as well, as multi-ethnic churches grow, and preachers talk more about the unity of the body of the Enemy.

However, we have powerful and influential allies who are aiding our cause. The media corporations, activists, and politicians on both extremes of the issues have discovered that there is great wealth and power in clicks, readership, and viewer ratings, which they are able to achieve when they create outrage. Therefore, there is wealth and power to be gained by pitting groups against each other so that everyone is offended and outraged at any perceived slight by another group. Our tempters have been quite successful in diminishing the appeal of the gospel of the Enemy by baiting Christians into frivolous debates with our allies, while those who have been marginalized, disenfranchised, and hurt are not being helped by either side. It is a beautiful spectacle to behold.

An essential foundational characteristic of an effective Christian leader is that they have a genuine interest in all people, that they value all people, and that they serve people without regard to nationality, gender, or race. You must undermine this foundation in your patients. Here, my dear Slugtoad, is where your youth and experience will be a disadvantage for you. While it is not difficult to prompt a hard-hearted person to act callously toward their fellow human, a wise tempter is able to manipulate a genuine heart that desires to serve others in the name of the Enemy and create hatred and bitterness to those who do not care or have a different perspective of how to accomplish the service.

In the past, we have seen great success in our efforts to devalue human life. Slavery, racism, and abortion have been universally effective in devaluing human life in nearly all cultures.

Regarding your patients, the man has developed deep friendships with his teammates and has become empathetic to the plight of those who feel marginalized because of their race. While this is unfortunate because of his ability to build relationships and bridges, as effective leaders do, you can use it to your advantage. The key is to persuade him to have a condescending and judgmental attitude toward the people who either do not care or believe there is a better way to solve the problem. This will cause the fire of racial division to be exacerbated instead of healed. The best ways to accomplish this is to keep him in a bubble of friends who are like him and to consume news that only confirms his bias and does not provide a thoughtful perspective of another point of view. This means he cannot be permitted to examine the plethora of scriptures of the Enemy that refer to unity in the body, loving your neighbor, racial harmony (Jews, Greeks, Samaritans, and more), etc.

In her role as team captain, the woman has begun to serve all the players on her team equally. It seems that she sees the value in each individual teammate. This must not stand. You must convince her to favor the followers who she likes and who are like her. If she realizes the power of this type of service in leadership, it will make your job more difficult when you try to convince her to relinquish this style as she leads larger groups of followers.

Serving all people equally begins with individual relationships and then builds to an organizational level. You must not allow your young patients to begin building those relationships and service.

Your affectionate uncle
MARDUK

4

Strong Work Ethic

MY DEAR SLUGTOAD,
You have done well in planting seeds of moral superiority in the minds of your patients while they surround themselves mostly with people who think like they do. This will make it difficult for them to value and serve people of other backgrounds. However, do not be overconfident. As they graduate and move from their college friends to their new jobs, they are vulnerable to becoming more open-minded.

As they start their new jobs and engage in church life as an adult, it is imperative that you discourage a strong work ethic. A strong work ethic leads to effective leadership. The Enemy exposed a secret of our Father Below: "Idle hands are the devil's workshop" (Prov. 16:27, TLB). Fortunately for you, our entertainment division has provided excellent resources for your use in this area. Your most effective tools are Netflix, Disney+, Hulu, HBO Max, and other streaming services. With these, you will be able to keep your patients distracted for extended periods, which keeps them from becoming engaged in leadership activities. When your patients start a family, make sure the children are promptly engaged in activities that require Sunday morning participation.

Your primary problem is going to be with the woman because she sees her work as ministry that is offered to the Enemy. If she maintains this perspective, it will be difficult to convince her that her work is drudgery to be avoided. Show her other women who are working less and seem to be accomplishing more. Comparison destroys contentment.

Your man is competitive and already has a strong work ethic, so use it to your advantage. Keep him focused on the successes of peers at work so that he is like a hamster in a wheel that eventually exhausts himself. Make sure he does not take vacations or other breaks so that he is eventually burned out. His relentless work in his career will keep him out of the leadership roles at churches, nonprofits, and even his family.

Your affectionate uncle
MARDUK

5

Integrity

M Y DEAR SLUGTOAD,
I will write today as if you are going to read and
heed my advice, although I must admit vexation at
your ineptitude. However, there is one ray of light. You said your
female seemed to be wrestling with an inner conflict. When she
was asked directly whether she agreed with the prevailing senti-
ment of the day that all men are oppressive in some way towards
women, she equivocated nicely. My educated guess is that she fears
rejection by the director of diversity at her company who posed
the question.

This is a great opportunity for you to redeem yourself. Continue to whisper in her ear of the necessity of pleasing people.
Make certain she understands the importance of a good reputation. Say it that way, because it sounds like something the Enemy
would say, but make sure what you are really teaching her is the art
virtue signaling. Social media is an excellent resource for examples
of that. Nothing is more exquisite than one who has fooled themselves into thinking that they are a good person, simply because
they have discovered how to agree with the majority in what they
say, while taking absolutely no action. If you fail in this, as you are
likely to do, at least continue to convince her to focus on her moral

superiority. I have no time to elaborate on that topic, but perhaps in my next letter.

The goal is to teach her how to talk a talk that is separated from her actual walk. I can hear you puzzling over this as I write it, so let me make it simple for you: I do not want her trusting her own integrity. First convince her to say or do something out of line with her convictions, then you must ever so subtly remind her of the fact that she has done so. *But do be vague*, for Lucifer's sake. If you are too direct and obvious, she will only repent of dishonesty with herself and others, and the last thing we need is for her to redouble her efforts to act like *Him*.

"Integrity" is a word that means *whole*, so what we want is the opposite. We want both of your charges to be fragmented. Remember our goal. We want them to be unfit for leadership, or if they are to lead, let them lead their followers to Our Father. Nothing accomplished this like duplicity. It has been those infernal men and women of integrity who have violated the darkness with so much light. It is a wonder we still have such an enormous foothold on the earth. Remember, truth and light are related. Snuff out truth with lies, and the darkness will be victorious.

Your affectionate uncle
MARDUK

6

Humble

MY DEAR SLUGTOAD,

In my last letter I mentioned briefly that you should continue to direct your female's attention to her own moral superiority. I wanted to say that the same instruction should be applied to the male. This, I must admit, has been a strong suit of yours dear nephew, but I am beginning to think it is your only skill. I will continue to write about the other "tools in your tool bag," but for today, I will focus on this strength of yours.

Though none of us can possibly understand the mind of the Enemy, it is certain there is very little that he values more. You will, of course, remember that it was our Father's very lack of humility that caused him to be elevated to his current position of Ruler of the Darkness. While I hesitate to want to see such a rise in station for your charges, remember that the most important thing is to bring them to enmity with our Enemy. The goal is separation above all else. Nothing drives a wedge like arrogance.

I have not forgotten your question. You asked why if arrogance is so important do I continue to berate you and "humble you" in my letters. But is that what I am doing? By your question I can see that you are anything but humble. In fact, hasn't my berating produced the opposite? Your arrogance and pride cause you to bristle under it. This gives me an idea for the man. You said he is excelling at work. I trust you obeyed me and distracted his mind with competitive thoughts toward his co-workers. Now you must collaborate with whomever oversees his direct superior in his company. Have him belittle your man just enough to enrage him, but not enough to make him question his life. As soon as his overlord does this, whisper to the man that he is ten times the worker that his manager is. It makes my blood boil deliciously just imagining the effect this will have on the man.

Oh, and this is of the utmost importance, *keep him away from his church*. I do not want him at worship service, at his men's study of that . . . that *book*. He must not get perspective from anyone who is wise. Rather, did you not say the sales department at his company is like a college fraternity? Keep him engaged with that sort. Whisper to him about some sort of Sunday sports league in which he can participate. I do not really care which tactic is used, but see that you do not fail.

Never forget what you learned in your training. We are always only one generation away from losing our foothold. The future depends on you, my dear Slugtoad—Dark Lord help us!

Your affectionate uncle
MARDUK

7

Servant Attitude

MY DEAR SLUGTOAD,
I will try from now on to make allowances for your limited mental capacity. I am afraid I have been too vague, having expected too much from you. I will try to spell it out in simple language from this point on, though this will be trying for my patience.

When I wrote to you about humility, I could see from your questions that you needed to be more specific. What I am trying to make your pea-sized brain comprehend is that if your charges develop what our enemies revere as a "servant attitude," you have great difficulty restraining them. If they learn the secret that serving others is the way to lead others to greatness, all will be lost. If the multiplicative effect of this type of leadership spreads to each successive generation, well, we cannot even speak of the impossibility of overcoming that disaster.

Now for the good news, dear nephew. The human heart is naturally repulsed by the idea of a servant attitude. Many of them aspire to be servant leaders until they are treated like a servant. Oh, they love to follow a leader with such an attitude, but to be such a leader defies their nature, at least where their nature is corrupted by the genius of Our Father in Hell.

There are many ways to distract them from even pretending such an attitude: one can whisper sweet lies of self-aggrandizement, one can draw their attention to their sense of victimhood, and one can surround them with thoughts of those to whom they feel superior.

All these methods are worth pursuing, but there is one thing that is of the utmost necessity. You must, and I cannot overstate this imperative, you *must* not allow your charges to consider that son of our Enemy. He is a chip off the old block if there ever was one. His very presence tortures the soul of the very best of us. He is powerful and to deny that is to evade unfortunate reality. So that is why it is incomprehensible to me that he would take the position that he is fond of, that of a servant. He made himself as low as possible. I am sure you have heard of his disgusting habit of serving what he calls, "the least of these." Pathetic. He even washed the filthy feet of our man Judas. *Judas!* If he will serve Judas, who will he not serve. Of course, we shall not even speak of our defeat in the greatest battle yet, the cross. As soon as the Dark Lord thought that he had won, he was nearly destroyed. If we are to recover from that, we absolutely must turn the eyes of humanity away from this. Pathetic as it is, it seems to be death to our cause. As these vermin "die to themselves," as they say, and adopt the attitude of a servant, they become almost impervious to our wiles. *Almost.* For while they are still bags of flesh in jars of clay, we can still get them distracted. There are many tools at your disposal, just pick one and try not to make a mess of it again. I do not mind warning you of the torture in store for you if you fail in this. I must admit, while your success is necessary, I do fantasize about the pain I will inflict on you if you give reason.

Your affectionate uncle
MARDUK

8

Intense Resolve

MY DEAR SLUGTOAD,
Well done. It pains me to say it, but anyone can see from what you have said that your man is merely faking his servant attitude. Look how upset he gets when his efforts go unnoticed. Your move to see that his coworker got the praise for something your charge accomplished was truly inspired. However, it brings up an important point. This sort of agony will produce one of two things in a man. The first possibility is what we want. We want him to give up trying. We want to drive him toward nihilism and apathy. Let him see first that servanthood is thankless and ineffective. Be sure to make him feel guilty about how angry he is at his lack of recognition. He will settle for mediocrity at best, and at worst he will shoot up a shopping mall. Oh, I know your man has not fallen that low, but what has been done before can be done again.

The second possibility comes with a slight danger but should not necessarily lead to total failure on your part. The second possibility is that your man develops an intense resolve. Thousands of the Enemy's children have been driven to succeed in doing something great by their insecurity and thirst for recognition. One can easily see the motive behind such resolve, and it will usually burn of the fruit. But still, others may learn the resolve by all the wrong motives; however, they will then purify their motives by some epiphany or cathartic experience of the Enemy or one of his messengers. The very last thing we want is to turn one of our most valued high-capacity assets into a force against us. All this is subtle, nuanced work, my dear nephew, and I doubt you are up to the task. Nevertheless, we are shorthanded just now, and you will have to do.

You see, *intense resolve* is something most humans lack. When I say most, I mean 99.67 percent (yes, the numbers are official). We have done an adequate job of surrounding them in comfort and stoking the fires of their appetites for pleasure and leisure. We have distracted them from the things that are most important in their tiny lives, and we have most recently upheld mediocrity as humility so that they are thoroughly confused in the issue.

While servant leadership can be effective for the Enemy, we have lured many servant leaders into ineffectiveness by mitigating their resolve. A servant leadership with no passion, resolve, or sense of mission is of little threat to us. It is when they combine the servant attitude with intense resolve that our cause is damaged.

But let me be clear, you are playing with fire (I mean that in the sense that the humans say it). If he learns intense resolve and it gets redeemed to the cause of our Enemy, he will not only be lost to you, but he will be destructive to us. Make no mistake, intense resolve is the difference between a man of noble character, and the same man storming the beautiful gates of Hell! I will write again on this topic from time-to-time to keep it fresh on your mind.

Your affectionate uncle
MARDUK

9

Genuine

M Y DEAR SLUGTOAD,
I had noticed your reticence regarding your female
patient, so I am glad you brought her up. Though I am
beginning to find you to be like a toilet plunger; you keep bringing
up old crap. Excuse my vulgarity, but sometimes vulgarity is the
only way to get through to the lower classes.

Your question belies your inability to understand the most
basic of concepts. When I wrote to you of integrity, you seemed to
have missed the point completely. If ignorance is bliss, you must
be overjoyed! Your female patient is on the verge of becoming
something dangerous to our cause. She is in danger of becoming
genuine. A genuine and authentic leader is able to relate to their
followers. You said you do not believe this to be a problem, but that
is only because you know nothing. You are right to disdain them,
but you are wrong to underestimate the harm they can cause. What
do you suppose it means for any one of them to become genuine?
It means they will drop all pretense. Who does pretense among
men serve? Is it our Lord or the Enemy? I will give you the benefit
of the doubt and assume your answer was the correct one. For the
Enemy's children to keep up appearances, to wear masks, to put on
a persona — these are all ways of saying the same thing — means
they believe fundamentally that there is something wrong with

them. They believe they could not be accepted just the way the Enemy has made them. And can one blame them? Not I. They are clumsily made. They are stupid, ugly, and weak. I too would wear a mask if I were one of them.

But that is not the way our Enemy has created them to flourish. He has made it easy. They simply are to "be." If they can just be with our Enemy, who has recklessly made a way for them to do just that, they have no reason to hide their true selves. Did you know that the first man and woman used to walk around in a paradisal garden in complete nakedness? I can already hear your brain about to explode in the attempt to grasp the meaning of this. I will help you. They had no shame! Can you imagine! The dark world runs on the shame of mankind. Our Lord was brilliant in his attack in the garden. Do you know what they did first? They made clothes and then they hid! Men have been hiding ever since.

This cannot be overstated. You must keep your woman away from the older lady in her church. That woman has caused us incredible harm, and from what you have written, she is lost to us completely. If she has a moment alone with her, she will fill her head with all manner of acceptance and what they call truth, but what I call nonsense. She will say the Enemy loves her and made her exactly how he wanted to. She will not even have to tell her to be genuine, she will simply become that way by default. And remember this, a leader who is genuine will gather more followers than one who is not. You must, MUST whisper to her about her flaws. Get someone to criticize her looks, her intellect, *whatever*. Just get her doubting herself and pretending to be someone else. For what it is worth, I do not think you are making the most efficient use of social media. We will talk about it another time. I am tired, and I doubt you can comprehend all of this anyway.

Your affectionate uncle
MARDUK

10

Driven by a Sense
of Higher Calling

M Y DEAR SLUGTOAD,
Your man's lack of a servant heart following your
attempt to apply my instruction continues to astound
me, especially considering how badly you have been missing each
opportunity. Discouraging your patient from attaining higher
purpose would be a wasted effort—too direct. He might notice
what you are doing. It is much more beneficial to fuel the ego and
get them focused on their own goals and plans. It is near futile to
eliminate a human soul's desire for something greater. But it is like
taking candy from a baby to twist the desires of the soul to never
be satisfied.

The Enemy would have these souls be selfless, seeking the
greater good and finding purpose in the charitable works they
might do for others. He would have them believe it leads to a great
satisfaction in life. A disgusting pursuit really, but with a little effort you can pervert the intentions of their hearts by spreading a
little praise on their actions until their motivation is no longer to
benefit their fellow man, but to chase the affirmation their souls
crave.

It is an interesting object, the heart of man. The Enemy
crafted it with an innate need for affirmation and connection.

These pathetic creatures believe it is so they can commune with him. They believe it reveals that they were created for a reason. It is your job to persuade them that their own purpose is the only purpose that matters. Give them a little water on the garden of deceit you sow. Let them settle into belief that they have the only answer the world needs. Convince them the only value they have in their world is if they have a large platform or following. Then inflate their sense of importance until they think serving one another is beneath their calling.

When they have gained a little success, heap on the shame that they are not doing enough. Plant a desire within them to get a bigger audience, a larger following. Persuade them that the larger the following they have, the higher their calling is. Then dangle a carrot in front of them, another soul to which to compare themselves.

You must never let your patients discover any type of fulfillment in serving others, what the vermin call, "servant leadership." In fact, even the slightest taste of the pleasure of serving their fellow man may be all it takes to destroy our plans entirely. If you sense they are experiencing this sort of enjoyment, you must act quickly. You can thwart the joy of the Enemy in a few ways. You can fuel the praise until it gives them the overinflated sense of self-importance. Or you can go in the other direction and plant seeds of doubt so they reflect on their actions and believe they should have done more. Point out the things they forgot or how they could have done better, then pile on shame for the failure.

We are counting on you to see this through, though we are not optimistic.

Your affectionate uncle
MARDUK

11

Self-Motivated

M Y DEAR SLUGTOAD,
One of our biggest tasks when dealing with our
patients is to keep them unmotivated, or better yet,
to allow them to be motivated by the wrong things. The Enemy
thinks they are smart, encouraging men and women to strive for
greatness without any need of reward or affirmation along the way.
It is a toxin that we cannot allow to exist, not for a single moment.

These so-called leaders are always learning and growing,
seeking ways to improve. They set goals and feel the reward just
from achieving that thing they set out to do. You will notice it right
away because it is despicable and will likely make you ill. They seem
genuinely happy when they set a goal and obtain it. They do not
need encouragement or rewards. You cannot allow this to happen.
This sort of behavior swells like a rising bread in a warm room. If
left unchecked, the leaven will become a noxious odor that will
draw other vermin in until you cannot stop the way it grows. But
you must be smart here. It is not enough to discourage them when
they do not achieve. These over-achievers even fuel themselves by
competing with themselves, *themselves!* They are always wanting
to do better each day for some unknown reason

Distractions! Throw as many as you can their way: worthy
pursuits, selfless acts, opportunities to serve, or even hobbies and

selfish goals. Get them to focus on other things or weigh them down with too many pursuits. Provide them with so many worthy causes they cannot possibly attain them all. Then drop in some external motivation, a reward of some kind that is irresistible. Study them, Slugtoad. Find out what makes them tick, that tempting morsel of materialism to which they absolutely cannot say no. Then tell them seductively they deserve that reward. Remind them of this at every turn. Each time they see others being rewarded; recall to their memory the prize they should be claiming.

It will not be easy. Anyone can see they are not so easily lured away by material things. I blame your ineptitude for this. Their entire drive to do anything exists simply because of their passion to do well. But if you find their weakness, you can use it against them and redeem your sorry performance.

Another well-used tactic is to point out to them how everyone else is receiving praise and promotion for the good they are doing. Take it slow, one step at a time. In the beginning it will appear as if they are genuinely happy for those around them who are excelling. But a little boost to their ego, a dash of self-pride and a heavy dose of comparison to others, and you will have them eating out of your hands. The only thing that will motivate them after that is fear. Fear of failure, fear of missing out, you name it, and they will be running scared.

Do not bugger this one up, Slugtoad. We cannot afford to have self-motivated souls out here fighting against everything we stand for. Hell forbid you fail. The consequences would be catastrophic.

Your affectionate uncle
MARDUK

12

Trust

M Y DEAR SLUGTOAD,
From the very start I had such low expectations
for you, yet even still you have managed to disappoint
me time and again. I begin to worry that my efforts with you have
been completely in vain. After all this time and energy I have invested into your training, you are still allowing your subjects to
form and build trust! I would ask if you can see how dangerous
a thing that is, but because trust is spreading at a horrifying rate
among them as I write this, it is obvious to me that this simple
fact has completely escaped you. So let me educate you before you
blunder even more spectacularly than you already have.

Servant leaders have this sickening disposition toward believing the best about people. This allows them to stay calm and
relaxed when delegating important tasks. Let me help you put the
pieces together: they *trust* the people who follow them. In case you
have not yet a grasp on the dire consequences of allowing this type
of leadership to spring up among them, I am going to spell it out
for you so simply that a child could comprehend it and hope that's
not still too much for you. One person can do the work of one
person. But a leader who trusts their followers can multiply their
workload infinitely. Their effectiveness explodes, simply because
they can give and receive trust.

And the appalling nature of trust does not end with delegation of tasks on the leader's end, oh no! Followers of trustworthy leaders just will not question the tasks they are given. Suspicion and pride, two of our most valuable weapons in the fight against the Enemy, are as effective as soup spoons in relationships built on trust. This means one leader on the side of the Enemy wields not only the manpower of themselves, but also that of all who follow them, who *trust* them, increasing their influence exponentially. It is crucial that we stymie the formation of trust among the Enemy's children before its effects are any more devastating to our cause than they already have been.

Be stealthy now. Sow seeds of doubt in the mind of every follower. Your man seems to have garnered the trust and respect of a small group. If you can manage to do this right, you will not only prevent that group from growing, but you will significantly decrease it and ideally break it apart entirely. Find a flaw in his character, something that makes his followers uncomfortable with unquestioningly obeying him, then tease it out of him at every chance. Goad them into making mistakes, and really have fun testing him. Watching them become less and less like the Enemy can be such a joy. This will remind his followers that he is no less human than they are (and how crippled and damaged they all are!), in turn reminding them how untrustworthy he is. Then do the same to him. Trust and faith go hand in hand, and the human capacity for faith is such a pitiful, weak thing that it should be a simple task to break a man's ability to trust if you target his faith. Seeing is believing, and you will show him exactly what to believe. Open his eyes to every flaw, mistake, and shortcoming of his followers. At every turn, point out the bad in others, and in a worried tone, speculate about whether, considering these imperfections, *these* people are quite equipped to do the Enemy's work. These measures should sufficiently limit the growth of trust.

But if you really want to nip this in the proverbial bud, you will draw on the leader's memories. Sift through his past until you find a time when someone let him down or broke his trust, then make it woefully obvious to him that his followers will turn out to be just the same. Every time they do something or display a trait even remotely like the person who broke his trust, play the moment of betrayal in his head again until he cannot disconnect the events in his mind. This should cause fear and anxiety, which, if you distract him from consulting with the Enemy about them, will do wonders for our little trust epidemic.

While, as I said, it is exceedingly disappointing that you have allowed this to become an issue, you should at least be able to fix it rather easily now that you've been made aware. Once you have successfully broken a patient's ability to trust one person, they will be naturally disposed toward a lack of trust in others. This means you only must get this right one time. Unfortunately, the fact that your man has been able to develop this amount of trust leaves me very little hope that you will be able to manage even that. If you get this situation back on track, you will truly shock me. But you might as well give it your all; it is not as if you can make the situation any worse than it already is.

Your affectionate uncle
MARDUK

13

Dedication to the Organization

M Y DEAR SLUGTOAD,
Has it occurred to you that the letters I am writing you were meant to teach you something, rather than just be your casual reading material? Or have I been wasting my time penning them? Because you clearly have not been heeding my instructions! I will say, though, that when you miss the mark, you miss spectacularly, and I do enjoy a good spectacle.

There is a cancer growing in the heart of the woman whom you oversee. It is reprehensible, and it needs to be rooted out immediately. Her determination to stay devoted and give whole-hearted commitment, even when it is difficult, is going to derail your efforts entirely. Your singular mission is to see that the patients under your charge do not form the symptoms of Level 5 leadership ability. How I miss believing that you could not be so blind as to miss this festering infection *right* beneath your nose!

These humans parade around with no shame, blatantly encouraging dedication and commitment to their organizations or causes over the interests of the self. When they commit acts of self-sacrifice and servitude for the sake of advancing the Enemy's agenda, their dedication is honored and rewarded. These sacrifices may seem like silly, harmless little acts of delusion to you, Slugtoad, since hard work in the name of a greater goal seems to be a capacity with which our Lord just did not endow you. But–and by now, dear nephew, this should not be news to you–you have entirely miscalculated the danger in allowing such a team spirit to flourish. Remember Babel? Our forces organized all of mankind to commit fully to *our* cause. They accomplished so much that the Enemy had to personally scatter them and confuse them with language barriers to prevent our plans from being established.

Complete dedication unifies their hearts and minds together toward a singular goal, creating a near unstoppable force. A movement of humans with their own interests entirely set aside is incredibly difficult to achieve, so we are not as thoroughly equipped against it as we could be here in Hell, and it would rattle our gates at minimum.

I can only pray to Satan that the gravity of what you have allowed to happen here has sunk in for you. Use that healthy sense of shame to energize your next steps, because while we do not like to let it happen on this scale, I have seen outbreaks of loyalty before, and there are ways to address it. Pepper your female charge's life with every single one of these options to ensure she does not dedicate her heart wholly. Throw a few distractions at her, things she knows are vitally important, but make sure the timing of those things are in direct conflict with essential organization functions. Distract her long enough while making that doctor's appointment for her child that she schedules it at the same time as her important organization meeting. Do this regularly enough, and she will begin to feel torn between her personal life and her commitment to the organization.

Next—and this will feel counterintuitive, but it is beautiful, the way it works—push her to be *so* committed, *so* involved in the organization (it helps to develop a little guilt about the needs of her personal life first) that she becomes burnt out, constantly stressed and tired because of the constant requests of the organization. Remind her that she has no time to pursue her own hobbies and desires, and make sure you keep anyone who would teach her how to balance her life far, far outside of her circle. Then offer opportunities for her to partake in the extracurricular activities she enjoys. You will really do well here if you can cause more schedule conflicts with these things, forcing her to choose. If she makes the wrong choice and denies herself, just stir up drama and stress at the organization event. It will make her wish she had just stayed home.

Finally, refer to my last letter and reveal every flaw of every leader in her organization. Point them out to her at every turn. If she sees how *human* they all are, how weak and frail and not at all like they claim to be–especially if you distract her from the fact that she is just as flawed; she will not want to be a part of it at all, let alone commit fully.

Do this correctly, Slugtoad. You do not want to see the havoc a soul that has dedicated themselves fully to the Enemy can wreak. Do not make me regret my patience with you.

Your affectionate uncle
MARDUK

14

Does Not Seek the Spotlight

MY DEAR SLUGTOAD,
Based on my observations of your recent work, it is astoundingly clear that the lights are on, but nobody is home. You are about as beneficial for the cause as a screen door on a submarine. And do not try to explain away what happened yet again. Excuses are like nostrils; everyone has a few. I am all for a rotten work ethic, but your lousy lying abilities are a disgrace to this family; do not air them out.

I should cut you a bit of slack, however, because humility is such a sneaky attribute; it can sneak past even seasoned warriors for our cause entirely unobserved, and that is the reason it is so destructive to our goals. The humble heart may be stirring up all types of trouble for our forces, but because it does not announce its talents or accomplishments or demand accolades, it continues to cause damage, unnoticed. The Enemy would like you to be so ignorant of this fact that you pass right over this weapon as if nothing is the matter.

Open your eyes! This should be an easy task, for so many of your patients love to be the center of attention and have all eyes on them. Your woman, however, is a crafty creature. She is content to remain hidden doing her deeds in private without admiration, attention, or praise. She is like an undiagnosed tumor in our plans, growing and spreading its malignancy until others turn and become like her. They will corrupt and spread corruption until we are bankrupt.

Must I reiterate your mission? She has advanced incredibly close to her goal of Level 5 leadership, because *you* overlooked her unbecoming lack of attention-seeking behavior.

The Enemy perverts the minds of his followers, telling them he is the true light and that seeking the spotlight is an atrocity. He fools them into thinking his praise is something worth having, and that a relationship with him is of more value than sweet, sweet human validation. It is your job to stir up loneliness and a need for attention. Plant thoughts of not being good enough and cause her to crave validation. Do this by comparison. Show her how others are being praised for their acts; whisper to her that if *they* deserve to be there, in the spotlight, she should have certainly been there by now. Comparison is a virtue we want to foster in our patients.

Better yet, pull some strings and just push her into the spotlight. Let her see how it makes her soul feel proud and full. Give her a taste of attention and glory, then remind her how it felt next time she is doing the Enemy's work. Yes, at first it may seem that she applies more effort toward doing the deeds of the Enemy, but her craving for that lovely feeling of all eyes on her, all voices saying, "well done," will eat at her until she *needs* it. This will cause her to seek it out, tainting her work for the Enemy, and maybe, if you are lucky, even cut corners or take credit where none is due because she just wants it so badly.

Our goal is to form her character after that of our most ignoble Father. His light never came from himself and was always a reflection of the Enemy. What a glorious sight it was to see him bask in stolen glory. Now, recreate that in your subjects, and you will have succeeded.

Your affectionate uncle
MARDUK

15

A Clear Catalyst in
Achieving Results

MY DEAR SLUGTOAD,
If ignorance is bliss, you must be overjoyed, you utter simpleton. I am quite certain you will fail, but I have one more task for you anyway. And make no mistake, this one is going to push you to your limit. In fact, it may just test everything we have covered so far. We have only got to take such drastic measures because you have failed in such a jaw-droppingly extravagant way, so please, please get it through your horned skull that dropping the ball at this point is really, really not acceptable.

During your oversight of these humans, change has occurred within the Enemy's ranks. Despite my efforts to teach you every foolproof technique in my arsenal, His leaders have organized and motivated His followers. We have seen drastic spikes in instances of humility, selflessness, trust building, and collaboration. These humans have become exceedingly big for their britches and have gained so much ground that to merely halt them now would do no good. They are wreaking havoc everywhere they go as you read this, encouraging others to join their ranks and be the change in the world. We must attempt to undo advancements they have made.

The best way to keep these humans from leading others toward advancement and change is to throw everything we have at them. Do it subtly, of course. Because this effort will be crucial to eliminating the threat, we must do so with the precision of a surgeon. It will look more like cutting out an infected tooth than the train wreck I have observed your previous tactics to be. Target the leaders. This will reduce the effort on your part because whatever the leader is or does will be replicated in the followers.

The leaders are not weak, nor are they ignorant to our ways. They have been through the rigors of our testing and have advanced through the ranks despite our best efforts. This will be a challenge like no other for you, Slugtoad, but you *must* prevail. Follow my carefully laid out plan instead of whiling away the hours doing whatever you were doing when you allowed this crisis to form under your very nose, and you have a chance at succeeding.

Weaken them first with temptation. Encourage them to feed their flesh, rather than their spirit, man. This will cause a lethargy, which will ideally cause them to fall spiritually ill. With temptations abounding, hit them in the knees and weaken their resolve by pushing their buttons. Make every silly little pet peeve they have sprout up around them in abundance, causing frustration and irritation. They are above this petty annoyance by now, or else they would not have gotten this far, so softening them up first with a little desire to serve the self is crucial. Throw in some doubt about their ability to lead and their followers' abilities in general, and you have a decent storm brewing.

Finally, once they are crippled, attack their faith in the mission ahead of them. Convince them through carefully executed lies that nothing will ever change, even if they do their part, even if every one of their followers does their part. Discourage them by reminding them of history, the times they have failed, the times their ancestors have failed. And if that is not quite enough, inform them of the sheer impossibility of the task ahead. They may change the world for one soul, but they will never be able to change a whole world full of souls!

I can explain this all to you over and over, Slugtoad, but I cannot understand it for you. It should be simple enough for a neanderthal–but I digress. Watch their every movement with the analytical eye I sincerely hope has been latent in you until now. Come fully armed to battle with every tactic I have taught you; you will need them all.

Your affectionate uncle
MARDUK

16

The Verdict

M Y DEAR SLUGTOAD,
         I would really love to see from your point of view
how things went this horribly wrong, but I cannot fit
my head that far up my rectum. I knew you would struggle; I just
could not have foreseen how utterly you would fail. You see, but
you do not observe. Otherwise, you would have learned *something*,
anything from my many communications to you.

Look at what has become of your patients! They are basking
in the success of overcoming all your temptations and assembling
their ranks against us. Their followers go willingly after the Enemy,
spreading their message further every day. Do you feel that Slugtoad? That scorching pain stems from the presence of our Enemy.
They have overcome and obtained Level 5 leadership, and the
Enemy is pleased with them. They have surpassed servant leadership and achieved that paradoxical blend of personal humility and
indomitable will. Do you know what this means, idiot nephew of
mine? Their humility and will have already begun to multiply to
everyone who follows them. They are becoming an unstoppable
force! If there were a prize awarded for the ineptest of all creatures,
you would without a doubt take first, second, and third place in a
sweeping victory.

You were unable to derail their resolve, and now, with the added strength of their commitment to the Enemy's organization, along with a genuine sense of higher purpose (disgusting), they will flourish. It will take a legion to fix what you have allowed to happen. The Enemy is celebrating while we scramble to regroup. This may well be the most breathtaking failure in the history of all time. It makes my blood stop boiling just *thinking* about it. It is torture enough knowing *one* of them succeeded to evade your tentacles, but to know they will impart their skill into the following generations sickens me to my core.

Oh, how I would love to watch the flames lick and devour your body. To indulge in that sight would give me great pleasure. And do not give me more "explanations." I will not engage in mental combat with the unarmed. All you had to do was season their thoughts with a little discouragement, doubt, confusion, and distraction. I must have completely overestimated your ability to understand the simplest of instructions. If a thought even crosses your mind, it is on a very lonely journey across a very barren wasteland. Your ineptitude really is astonishing. The amount of time and energy that was poured into you only to result in this outcome is difficult to comprehend, let alone stomach.

The outcome of your ineptitude is to enroll in Tempters Training College again as a freshman. The work of tempting leaders of the Enemy is far too important to entrust to a rookie again.

Your affectionate uncle
MARDUK

Section 2

The Model

17

Leadership

ONE OF THE GREAT MYTHS of our culture is that leadership is associated with rank, title, or position.[1] When speaking to a group of students or adults on the topic of leadership, I sometimes begin by saying: "If you consider yourself a leader, please raise your hand." There is usually a period of uncertainty, and a couple of people will raise their hands. The uncertainty is understandable because there are numerous definitions of leadership, and most people consider only people in positions of authority to be the leaders. They usually think of politicians, bosses, or people with large platforms. However, when I share that my favorite definition of a leader is anyone who influences the thoughts and behaviors of other people, then almost every hand goes up. They realize that we all have situations where we lead, whether it is at work, at church, in the community, with friends, or within our family. The truth is that all of us influence the thoughts and behaviors of others, so a study of effective leadership is appropriate and desirable for everyone.

There is a leadership tension in modern culture between those who believe leadership is derived from the power of a position and those who believe that leadership is influence that is earned from followers. The legacy of positional power is persistently retaining control of many organizations, even though research shows that

1. Kouzes and Posner, "Finding Your Voice."

organizations utilizing humble leaders who seek the greater good are significantly more successful both for the organization and for individual leaders.[2] Kenneth Blanchard is well known for his best-selling books *The One Minute Manager*[3] and *Lead Like Jesus*,[4] and he summarizes today's leadership challenge well: "The key to successful leadership today is influence, not authority. . . . In the past, a leader was a boss. Today's leaders must be partners with their people. . . . they no longer can lead solely based on positional power."[5] Pause and read that again slowly. There is a key distinction between leadership that draws followers, and authority that is derived from a position or title.

Humility is the most underrated characteristic of leadership, and it may be the most important because it is a key ingredient that leads to the development of future generations of effective leaders and enduringly great organizations. This is not a new concept. Long before Greenleaf wrote about servant leadership[6] or Collins wrote about Level 5 leadership,[7] Socrates and Aristotle wrestled with the idea of humility in leadership,[8] Jesus admonished his disciples to be servants (Matt. 20:26, Mark 9:35, John 13), and Augustine wrote the *City of God* "to convince the proud of the power and excellence of humility."[9]

In the plethora of books, journal articles, blogs, conferences, seminars, and YouTube videos on the topic of leadership, there are a variety of ways leaders are evaluated and categorized. While acknowledging the numerous useful approaches to successful

---

2. Sisodia, "Servant Leadership Is Conscious Leadership"; Sisodia, "Understanding the Performance Drivers of Conscious Firms"; Reid, "Service and Humility in Leadership: Intriguing Theories, but Do They Actually Produce Results?," 2017; Collins, *Good to Great*.

3. Blanchard and Johnson, *The New One Minute Manager*.

4. Blanchard and Hodges, *Lead Like Jesus Revisited*.

5. Glover, Glover, and Glover, "The Power of Partners."

6. Greenleaf, "The Servant as Leader (an Essay)."

7. Collins, *Good to Great*.

8. Bobb, *Humility*.

9. Augustine, *City of God*.

leadership, it seems that the most useful approach for today's leaders is the distinction between positional leadership that is based on the power and ego of the leader and a variety of leadership styles that are anchored in a type of humility in the leader that seeks the good of others and does not rely on the power of the position or title of the leader. These leadership styles that seek the good of others are known by a variety of constructs and streams of leadership study and research including transformational, authentic, servant, and Level 5.

Leaders are especially effective when their humility is combined with a passion and zeal for a cause. Humble leaders often channel their energy into serving their followers. Therefore, this book focuses on Level 5 and servant leadership, which both begin with humility as a foundation. In addition, it is appropriate to consider transformational leadership since it is the most widely studied and has been shown to be a successful type of leadership.

18

The Difference Between
Leadership and Authority

THE DESIRE FOR GOOD LEADERSHIP, using influence to lead rather than authority to force, is seen in the abundance of material available to advocate for leadership principles. Although the idea of service and humility in leadership in Western culture is significantly influenced by the teachings of Jesus and the Christian heritage, it is interesting to note that most of the research and quotes referenced in this book originated from business, academic, political, and military sources, and not the church. In other words, this is not a study isolated to religion, but has been proven to be a study of human behavior that is consistent with Biblical teaching.

The concepts advocated by leadership development material can be summarized by quotes from well-known leaders. Here are some brief quotes that provide a sampling of the best insights into the humility, service, authority, and zeal of leadership, showing that leadership is not about positional authority.[1]

- Humility
  o A leader is best when people barely know he exists. When his work is done, his aim fulfilled, they will say: we did it ourselves. —Lao Tzu

1. Kruse, "100 Best Quotes on Leadership."

- o He who has never learned to obey cannot be a good commander. —Aristotle

- o I start with the premise that the function of leadership is to produce more leaders, not more followers. —Ralph Nader

- o No man will make a great leader who wants to do it all himself, or to get all the credit for doing it. —Andrew Carnegie

- o It is absurd that a man should rule others, who cannot rule himself. —Latin Proverb

- o It is better to lead from behind and to put others in front, especially when you celebrate victory when nice things occur. You take the front line when there is danger. Then people will appreciate your leadership. —Nelson Mandela

- o Leadership and learning are indispensable to each other. —John F. Kennedy

- o Education is the mother of leadership. —Wendell Willkie

- o A good leader is a person who takes a little more than his share of the blame and a little less than his share of the credit. —John Maxwell

- o There are three essentials to leadership: humility, clarity and courage. —Fuchan Yuan

- o My responsibility is getting all my players playing for the name on the front of the jersey, not the one on the back. —Unknown

- Service
  - o The first responsibility of a leader is to define reality. The last is to say thank you. In between, the leader is a servant. —Max DePree

  - o Before you are a leader, success is all about growing yourself. When you become a leader, success is all about growing others. —Jack Welch o To command is to serve, nothing more and nothing less. —Andre Malraux

o The best executive is the one who has sense enough to pick good men to do what he wants done, and self-restraint enough to keep from meddling with them while they do it. —Theodore Roosevelt

o Outstanding leaders go out of their way to boost the self-esteem of their personnel. If people believe in themselves, it's amazing what they can accomplish. —Sam Walton

o As we look ahead into the next century, leaders will be those who empower others. —Bill Gates

o Leadership is unlocking people's potential to become better. —Bill Bradley

o The growth and development of people is the highest calling of leadership. —Harvey Firestone

o True leadership lies in guiding others to success. In ensuring that everyone is performing at their best, doing the work they are pledged to do and doing it well. —Bill Owens

o The greatest leader is not necessarily the one who does the greatest things. He is the one that gets the people to do the greatest things. —Ronald Reagan

- Authority
  o You don't need a title to be a leader. –Multiple Attributions

  o Become the kind of leader that people would follow voluntarily, even if you had no title or position. —Brian Tracy

  o You manage things; you lead people. —Rear Admiral Grace Murray Hopper

  o A leader takes people where they want to go. A great leader takes people where they don't necessarily want to go, but ought to be. —Rosalynn Carter

- o Leadership is the art of getting someone else to do something you want done because he wants to do it. —General Dwight Eisenhower

- o He who has great power should use it lightly. —Seneca

- o You don't lead by hitting people over the head—that's assault, not leadership. –Dwight Eisenhower

- o A great leader's courage to fulfill his vision comes from passion, not position. —John Maxwell

- o In matters of style, swim with the current; in matters of principle, stand like a rock. —Thomas Jefferson

- o Management is about arranging and telling. Leadership is about nurturing and enhancing. —Tom Peters

- o Management is efficiency in climbing the ladder of success; leadership determines whether the ladder is leaning against the right wall. —Stephen Covey

- Zeal / Passion / Influence
  - o My own definition of leadership is this: The capacity and the will to rally men and women to a common purpose and the character which inspires confidence. —General Montgomery

  - o Leadership is lifting a person's vision to high sights, the raising of a person's performance to a higher standard, the building of a personality beyond its normal limitations. —Peter Drucker

  - o Effective leadership is not about making speeches or being liked; leadership is defined by results not attributes. —Peter Drucker

  - o Leadership is influence. —John C. Maxwell

  - o If your actions inspire others to dream more, learn more, do more and become more, you are a leader. —John Quincy Adams

o You don't lead by pointing and telling people some place to go. You lead by going to that place and making a case. —Ken Kesey

o Great leaders are not defined by the absence of weakness, but rather by the presence of clear strengths. —John Zenger

o Lead and inspire people. Don't try to manage and manipulate people. Inventories can be managed but people must be led. —Ross Perot

o Leaders must be close enough to relate to others, but far enough ahead to motivate them. —John C. Maxwell

o Leadership is solving problems. The day soldiers stop bringing you their problems is the day you have stopped leading them. They have either lost confidence that you can help or concluded you do not care. Either case is a failure of leadership. —Colin Powell

o No man is good enough to govern another man without that other's consent. —Abraham Lincoln

o The final test of a leader is that he leaves behind him in other men, the conviction and the will to carry on. —Walter Lippman

o The greatest leaders mobilize others by coalescing people around a shared vision. —Ken Blanchard

o To do great things is difficult; but to command great things is more difficult. —Friedrich Nietzsche

o To have long term success as a coach or in any position of leadership, you have to be obsessed in some way. —Pat Riley

o Whatever you are, be a good one. —Abraham Lincoln

o A cowardly leader is the most dangerous of men. —Stephen King

o Earn your leadership every day. —Michael Jordan

19

Level 5 Leadership

LEVEL 5 LEADERSHIP WAS IDENTIFIED, and the term coined, by Jim Collins in *Good to Great*,[1] one of the best-selling and most influential business books in history.[2] The popularity of the book was boosted beyond the typical audience for business books, so that at least half of the books were sold to purchasers outside of the typical audience of business book purchasers,[3] with church leaders being the largest non-business audience.[4] The primary appeal outside of the business market was primarily due to the chapter on Level 5 leadership, which described effective leaders as having a paradoxical blend of *personal humility* and *professional will*. In addition to successful outcomes, there are two aspects of Level 5 leadership that intrigue people in all types of organizations: 1) success is not based on genes, so that anyone with humility and zeal can be an effective leader and 2) it is consistent with leadership teachings and examples of the Bible.[5] It is ironic that the results of this secular research of American corporations has identified the

1. Collins, *Good to Great*.
2. Leighton, "The 31 Most Influential Books Ever Written about Business."
3. Bryant, "For This Guru, No Question Is Too Big."
4. Maney, "True Believers Ignite Super Sales Rate for 'Good to Great.'"
5. Maney, "True Believers Ignite Super Sales Rate for 'Good to Great.'"

type of modern leadership that is arguably the most aligned with Biblical teaching and modeling.[6]

The research question that drove the research that resulted in *Good to Great* was: "Is it possible for a company that has been good for a long time, to become great?"[7] Collins and his research team examined stock returns of 1,435 publicly traded companies between 1965 and 1995 and identified 11 that had been good companies for a long time but then suddenly became great, as evidenced by suddenly outperforming their industries and comparable companies by orders of magnitude. The research team discovered that the CEOs of all 11 great companies manifested an unusual combination of personal humility and professional will that was lacking in the CEOs of the comparison companies.[8] Unfortunately, it is the outspoken and not-so-humble Level 4 leaders who draw the attention and provide the visible model for young leaders to follow.[9] Therefore, the humble and zealous Level 5 leaders tend to be overlooked in the shadow of the larger-than-life leaders.

As Collins' research team was searching for a term to describe this new type of leadership seen in the good-to-great companies, there was discussion regarding calling it "servant leadership." However, according to Collins, members of the team violently objected to these characterizations. "Those labels don't ring true. . . . It makes them sound weak or meek, but that is not at all the way that I think of [these leaders]. They would do almost anything to make the company great." [10] The Collins team noted the extensive literature regarding levels of executive capabilities, which they identified as levels one through four.[11] They finally decided just to call this new fifth level of leader a Level 5 executive.

In teaching students and working with Christian leaders on the topic of Level 5 leadership, I have found Collins' term

6. Reid, *Zervant Leadership - Because Servant Leadership Is Not Enough.*

7. Collins, *Good to Great*

8. Collins, *Good to Great.*

9. Penn Wharton School, "Good Vs. Great Leaders."

10. Collins, *Good to Great*, 30.

11. Collins, *Good to Great.*

professional will a bit clunky and difficult to use. When people hear that term, they often get a vague understanding of what is intended but are not sure of its precise meaning. Nearly 20 years after *Good to Great* was published, Collins seemed to encounter similar feedback and changed the terminology on his web site and his latest book to *indomitable will* instead of professional will.[12] Indomitable is defined as "impossible to subdue or defeat,"[13] which provides a much clearer description of the will that is exhibited by Level 5 leaders. Therefore, the term *professional will* shall be replaced by *indomitable will* for the remainder of this book.

The next chapters will explore the ten attributes in the Level 5 Leadership Scale (L5LS), organized by the constructs of personal humility and indomitable will. Each attribute will be examined in the context of leadership theory and practice.

---

12. Collins, "Concepts - Level 5 Leadership"; Collins and Lazier, *BE 2.0 (Beyond Entrepreneurship 2.0)*, 155.

13. "Oxford Dictionary on Lexico.Com."

20

Characteristics of Level 5 Leaders

The Level 5 Leadership Scale (L5LS)

THERE HAS BEEN LITTLE EMPIRICAL RESEARCH on Level 5 leadership because there was not a validated instrument, or survey, to measure it for over a decade. Collins described what it looked like but did not describe how to measure it. In fact, one of the critiques of Level 5 leadership is that Collins himself could not always identify if a leader, even one he was very familiar with, was Level 5.[1]

The purpose of my dissertation in 2012 was to develop a validated instrument that could be used to research Level 5 leadership.[2] To do this, all the 99 attributes that Collins used to describe Level 5 leaders were compiled, and a panel of experts who had published articles about Level 5 leadership refined the list to 74 attributes. An online survey was developed that included the 74 attributes, and 349 participants evaluated their bosses on a 10-point semantic differential scale for each attribute. In addition, Collins proposed eight untested questions to determine if an individual is Level 5,

---

1. May, "'Good to Great' Review."
2. Reid, "Development of an Instrument to Measure Level 5 Leadership."

so those eight questions were also included.[3] The results showed that there are two very distinct constructs within the 74 attributes that match Collins' proposed personal humility and indomitable will constructs and explain a statistically significant 55.2% of the variance within the attributes. The final scale contains five attributes of personal humility and five attributes of indomitable will. Reliability is very good with Cronbach's alpha of .833 and .845 respectively. The analysis also showed that there is a statistically significant positive relationship between the Level 5 attributes and Collins' eight questions. The final validated instrument is shown below:

Level 5 Leadership Scale (L5LS)

On a scale of 1 to 10, to what extent do the following characteristics describe the subject? A one indicates that this characteristic does not describe him/her at all, while a ten indicates that it describes him/her exactly.

Personal Humility

- Humble
- Genuine
- A team player
- Servant attitude
- Doesn't seek the spotlight

Indomitable Will

- Intense resolve
- Dedication to the organization

3. Collins, "Where Are You on Your Journey from Good to Great? Good to Great Diagnostic Tool."

- A clear catalyst in achieving results

- Strong work ethic

- Self-motivated

An average score of at least 7.5 on BOTH personal humility and indomitable will indicate that the subject is a Level 5 leader.[4]

It is important to note that the subject must score at least 7.5 out of the ten-point scale to be considered a Level 5 leader. There are common stereotypes of arrogant business leaders who have indomitable will or humble pastors who do not accomplish much. These characteristics must be seen in action working together to be considered a Level 5 leader.

Personal Humility

Collins identified the first construct of Level 5 leadership as personal humility.[5] To define humility, he simply described what it looked like in some of the CEOs that led their organizations to greatness. He described Darwin Smith of Kimberly-Clark as a shy man who lacked any pretense or air of self-importance. Smith reportedly felt unqualified to accept the job of CEO, and at his retirement 20 years later, he said that "he never stopped trying to become qualified for the job."[6] Colman Mockler, CEO of Gillette, was described as a quiet, reserved, courteous, gracious gentleman, with a placid persona. David Maxwell (Fannie Mae) was an advocate first and foremost for the company and not for himself. The lifestyle of Ken Iverson (Nucor) was simple, humble, and modest. The Level 5 leaders did not talk about themselves, and when others talked about them, they said it was not false modesty. They used words like "quiet, humble, modest, reserved, shy, gracious, mild mannered, self-effacing, understated, did not believe his own

---

4. Reid, "Development of an Instrument to Measure Level 5 Leadership."

5. Collins, *Good to Great*.

6. Spector, *Shared Values*, 10.

clippings; and so forth."[7] Additionally, he categorized Level 5 leaders as selfless, servant leaders.

Although people in the organization, as well as outside observers, credited the Level 5 leaders as the key to elevating their companies from good to great, these leaders did not accept the credit and often credited luck. Collins summarized a Level 5 leader as one who

> demonstrates a compelling modesty, shunning public adulation; never boastful . . . Acts with quiet, calm determination; relies principally on inspired standards, not inspiring charisma, to motivate . . . Channels ambition into the company, not the self; sets up successors for even greater success in the next generation . . . Looks out the window, not in the mirror, to apportion credit for the success of the company—to other people, external factors, and good luck.[8]

Within the personal humility construct of the L5LS, there are five attributes that describe Level 5 leaders. While it might seem obvious that being humble is part of personal humility, the description of these Level 5 leaders incorporated concepts that went beyond simply being humble. Personal humility was also exemplified in the leaders through being genuine, being a team player, having a servant attitude, and not seeking the spotlight.

Humble

The idea that a leader should be humble originated millennia before Collins wrote *Good to Great*. Lao Tzu, a Chinese philosopher who taught around the 4th–6th century BC, said that before a person can become a leader of others, they must first avoid putting themselves before their followers by being a humble and supportive resource.[9] In the same era in Greece, Aristotle advocated a

---

7. Collins, *Good to Great*, 27.
8. Collins, *Good to Great*, 36.
9. Tzu, *The Complete Works of Lao Tzu*.

different approach: the magnanimous man. Magnanimity is when a great leader has a proper estimation of himself (since this virtue was the domain of war and politics, it was reserved only for men).[10] It is a balance between vanity, which is thinking of oneself too highly, and pusillanimity, which is thinking of oneself too lowly and could be described as timid or cowardly.[11] Aristotle's magnanimous man does not admit any deficiencies and is not reliant on anyone, which means that any humility on his part would deny his own magnanimity. Thereafter, leaders after Aristotle, including his pupil Alexander the Great, would not have the humility to see others as their equals.[12]

Therefore, the teachings of Jesus a few hundred years later were revolutionary. Humility is taught and modeled throughout the New Testament by Jesus, Paul, Peter, and others (Matt. 23:10-12, Luke 14:11, John 13, 1 Peter 5:5-6, Phil. 2:1-11, 2 Cor. 4:5, Col, 3:12, Eph 4:2, James 4:6-10, Romans 12:3). Since there is a strong correlation between humble leaders and servant leaders, the scriptural examples are explored further in the chapter about servant leadership.

After the fall of Rome in the early 5th century, the early church father Augustine wrote that a Christian prince who would lead should reorder the hierarchy of virtues so that humility is elevated to the highest rank.[13] Aristotle's magnanimous man and Augustine's Christian prince both accomplish great things, but their motivation and means to accomplish the ends are very different. In the 13th century, Thomas Aquinas combined these ideas and claimed that magnanimity and humility should not be considered opposing virtues, but complementary.[14] Aquinas argues that a magnanimous person who has a deference before God is more attentive to the needs of others and more capable of fulfilling them. By repositioning Aristotle's idea of magnanimity so that the leader

10. Bobb, *Humility*.

11. Bobb, *Humility*.

12. Bobb, *Humility*.

13. Augustine, *City of God*.

14. Bobb, *Humility*.

retains a correct estimation of himself in relation to God and his fellow man, the leader has the critical balance of self-confidence to strive for ambitious and worthy objectives and the humility to listen to others and to serve followers.

Although the support for humble leaders has ancient origins, is attractive in theory, and elicits substantial lip service, many people do not believe it will lead to successful outcomes in practice. To understand the concept of humility in leadership, it is necessary to understand what humility is not. A humble leader is sometimes mistakenly believed to be simply a compliant conformist who perpetuates the status quo.[15] Many people see humility as being a doormat for others to walk over, but "true humility is not thinking less of yourself; it's thinking of yourself less."[16] C.S. Lewis wrote that truly humble people are not ones who think of themselves as nobody, but ones who understand that all have pride and that they generally do not even think about humility because they don't think of themselves at all.[17] In other words, humble people shouldn't be seen as inept and worthless people with an accurate view of themselves, they should be seen as strong people who are self-aware to know their strengths and weaknesses, but their focus is on an organization, a cause, or other people and not themselves.

Therefore, humble leaders are not simply shy, timid doormats with poor self-esteem. Collins concluded that humility serves as a key to successful leadership, since "we cannot see something from the perspective of another if we do not have deep humility, because without it we impose our own perspective or analyze things from our own perspective only; we will not see the other person's viewpoint."[18] Similarly, leaders must reassess their roles regarding practice and power within the organization, and the organization must consider whether their leaders recognize and appreciate the

---

15. Kalina, "False Humility: The Plague of Genuine Leadership."

16. Warren, *The Purpose Driven Life*.

17. Lewis, *Mere Christianity*.

18. Serfontein and Hough, "Nature of the Relationship between Strategic Leadership, Operational Strategy and Organisational Performance," 396.

implications of their power.[19] The key reason humility is effective in leadership is that humble leaders realize they do not have all the answers, so they surround themselves with bright people who will provide candid feedback. This diversity of viewpoints and opinion leads to stronger leadership and enables the development of other leaders.

Collins said that it would be a mistake to think of the humility of these Level 5 leaders as weakness. In fact, he said their humility was the opposite of weakness because they focused all their attention on the organization or the cause instead of themselves.[20] Level 5 leaders are often radical in their obsession to make the organizations great.

Genuine

True humility is a noble pursuit for leaders, but a forced or false humility is detrimental to effective leadership.[21] False humility is a deceptive, self-serving façade. Therefore, the attitude and personal humility of Level 5 leaders is genuine, which means the leaders relate authentically with their followers. Leaders who are genuine can develop relationships with their followers because the authenticity allows them to be approachable. In leadership research and studies, the characteristics of a genuine leader have been conceptualized as authentic leadership.[22]

The idea of genuineness or authenticity is rooted in Greek philosophy and developed in modern times by humanistic psychologists such as Rogers and Maslow, with a focus on the fully functioning or actualized individual being able to see their basic nature clearly and accurately.[23] Maslow notes that self-actual-

19. Goleman, "Leadership That Gets Results."

20. Jim Collins, "From Good to Great: What Defines a Level V Leader?" 2009, https://www.youtube.com/watch?v=q-KyQ9oXByY&t=1s.

21. Kalina, "False Humility: The Plague of Genuine Leadership."

22. Avolio and Gardner, "Authentic Leadership Development."

23. Avolio and Gardner, "Authentic Leadership Development."

ized people who are genuine and authentic have strong ethical convictions.[24]

Authentic leaders foster the development of authentic followers through four distinct activities: self-awareness, balanced processing, relational transparency, and authentic behavior.[25] Self-awareness indicates that leaders can see their own character, desires, feelings and motives clearly and objectively through introspection and reflection. By first being self-aware, the leader is then able to relate authentically with others. Balanced processing recognizes that while everyone has biases, an authentic leader has the ability and the inclination to consider multiple sides of an argument and assess the information fairly. Relational transparency reflects the willingness of the leader to share information openly and transparently with others. Finally, authentic behavior provides a positive model for followers to emulate so they are developed as authentic leaders. Authentic leaders exhibit self-transcendent values that are universally valued, such as justice, honesty, loyalty, responsibility, gratitude, and concern for others.[26]

Interestingly, authentic and transformational leadership are linked so that authentic leadership leads to transformational changes in followers.[27] Transformational leadership contrasts with transactional leadership and laissez-faire leadership in the full range leadership model.[28] Transformational leaders are able to relate to their followers personally and motivate their followers to strive for a mission or purpose that is greater than themselves. They must be authentic, turn followers into leaders, and rally their followers to a cause that is greater than themselves. Christian leaders have a common cause as they point their followers to Christ.

24. Maslow, *The Farther Reaches of Human Nature.*

25. Avolio and Gardner, "Authentic Leadership Development."

26. Avolio and Gardner, "Authentic Leadership Development."

27. Banks, McCauley, Gardner, and Guler, "A Meta-Analytic Review of Authentic and Transformational Leadership: A Test for Redundancy."

28. Reid, "The Mind of the Transformational Leader."

A Team Player

In addition to the conclusion that being a team player is a key for Level 5 leaders.[29] Common sense and scholarly research studies also state that teamwork is critical to achieving success.[30] In his book, *The Ideal Team Player*, Patrick Lencioni identified three key virtues that are exhibited in an ideal team player: humble, hungry, and smart.[31] The importance of being humble has been addressed, but in the context of being a team player it is the characteristic that allows the leader to share credit with teammates and emphasize the team over the individual. Being hungry is the indomitable will, zeal, passion, and intensity that is addressed in the next section. This leaves the perplexing characteristic of being *smart*.

Lencioni clarifies that the idea of being smart is not about cognitive intelligence, but about the common sense of dealing with people. He states that this is often referred to as emotional intelligence, which is supported by extensive research in leadership.[32] Emotional intelligence is defined as "the capacity to be aware of, control, and express one's emotions, and to handle interpersonal relationships judiciously and empathetically."[33] Emotional intelligence is positively correlated with servant leadership.[34] In his ground-breaking book, *Emotional Intelligence: Why It Can Matter More than IQ*, Daniel Goleman found that emotional intelligence was a crucial characteristic of effective leaders, and he identified five components:

1. Self-awareness: understanding self, strengths and weaknesses, and the impact these have on others

---

29. Collins, *Good to Great*.

30. Rezvani, Barrett, and Khosravi, "Investigating the Relationships among Team Emotional Intelligence, Trust, Conflict and Team Performance."

31. Lencioni, *The Ideal Team Player*.

32. Lee, "Emotional Intelligence."

33. "Oxford Dictionary on Lexico.Com."

34. Lee, "Emotional Intelligence."

2. Self-regulation: the ability to control emotions and think before acting

3. Empathy: how well other people's viewpoints are understood and considered

4. Social skills: communicating and relating to others

5. Motivation: the drive to work and succeed.[35]

Being a team player and exhibiting emotional intelligence when dealing with other people are often aided by an understanding of personality types. Personality types are about preferences and tend to be fixed. Emotional intelligence is about competence and can be changed. Therefore, it is important to develop the ability to work and communicate well with others to be an effective team player.

A Servant Attitude

Maintaining a servant attitude begins with personal humility. This component of Level 5 leadership is addressed extensively in the chapter on servant leadership, so at this point it will just be mentioned as one of the five key components of the personal humility construct of Level 5 leadership.

Does Not Seek the Spotlight

Although the *spotlight* may be a charmingly dated metaphor, it provides an image of a person who draws attention. In today's world, the spotlight may be described as a platform that encompasses social media, blogs, website, books, and public speaking. Since leadership is the ability to influence the thoughts and behaviors of others, it seems that having a large platform, and therefore a large spotlight, would be beneficial for effective leadership. However, the size of the spotlight or platform is not the issue. The issue lies in where the spotlight is pointed.

35. Goleman, *Emotional Intelligence.*

Collins described the difference of focus by using the analogy of a window and a mirror. When the Level 5 leaders faced failure, they looked in the mirror and took responsibility for the failure. When achieving success, they looked out the window at the people who contributed to the success and gave them credit.

> Level 5 leaders look out the window to apportion credit to factors outside of themselves when things go well (and if they cannot find a specific person or event to give credit to, they credit good luck). At the same time, they look in the mirror to apportion responsibility, never blaming luck when things go poorly.[36]

While trying to avoid becoming political, the most obvious and recognizable modern example of this concept is Donald Trump. When things went well, such as the economy, foreign relations, and the Covid vaccine, he was quick to take credit. For example, "I am the only person in the history of our country that could really decimate ISIS."[37] However, when things did not go well, he blamed someone else. He once famously said "I don't take responsibility at all."[38] As former president Obama summarized: President Trump "takes responsibility for nothing but takes credit for everything."[39] Whether or not he deserved credit or blame for the variety of successes and failures is open for debate but misses the point. Level 5 leaders do not put the spotlight on themselves, except to accept responsibility for failures.

Indomitable Will

Ten years after the publication of *Good to Great*, Collins acknowledged that his description of Level 5 leaders "focused heavily on

---

36. Collins, *Good to Great*, 35.

37. Washington Post, *Trump Will Claim Credit for (Almost) Anything*.

38. Phillips, "Analysis | Everyone and Everything Trump Has Blamed for His Coronavirus Response."

39. Moreno, "Obama."

the humility aspect."[40] However, he and Hanson further concluded that the most important trait of Level 5 leaders is that they serve as "incredibly ambitious, but their ambition is first and foremost for the cause, for the company, for the work, not themselves."[41] Although Collins and secondary writers have dwelt more on personal humility in leaders because it seems to appear as a novel concept in the corporate world, Level 5 leadership presents as equal parts humility and "ferocious resolve, an almost stoic determination to do whatever needs to be done to make the company great."[42] After describing Darwin Smith's personal humility, Collins stated, "if you were to think of Darwin Smith as somehow meek or soft, you would be terribly mistaken. His awkward shyness and lack of pretense was coupled with a fierce, even stoic resolve toward life."[43] He coupled this intense, ferocious resolve with an incredible work ethic. Likewise, he described Colman Mockler as a strong and tireless fighter with an inner intensity to make whatever he touched the best it could be. He categorized David Maxwell as ambitious for the company and not himself. In that regard, he said: "Level 5 leaders are fanatically driven, infected with an incurable need to produce results."[44] Level 5 leaders have a workmanlike diligence. They serve as clear catalysts in the transitions from good to great, and they set the standard of greatness. They will settle for nothing less. Collins described indomitable will as "an absolute, obsessed, burning, compulsive ambition . . . that is not about them."[45]

The best term to encapsulate all the meaning in this description is the word *zeal*. Zeal is defined as "great energy or enthusiasm in pursuit of a cause or an objective"[46] or "fervor, passion, intense driving feeling and conviction, deep desire or coveting, and intense

40. Collins and Hansen, *Great by Choice*, 32.

41. Collins and Hansen, *Great by Choice*, 32.

42. Collins, *Good to Great*, 30.

43. Collins, *Good to Great*, 18.

44. Collins, *Good to Great*, 30.

45. Jim Collins, "From Good to Great: What Defines a Level V Leader?" 2009, https://www.youtube.com/watch?v=q-KyQ9oXByY&t=1s.

46. "Oxford Dictionary on Lexico.Com."

heat."[47] Although the terms *professional will* or *indomitable will* are not found in scripture, zeal in leadership is advocated. Christians with the spiritual gift of leadership are admonished to lead with zeal and never to be lacking in zeal (Rom. 12:6-11). When Jesus cleared out the money changers from the temple, his disciples remembered that it was written that "zeal for your house will consume me" (John 2:17). Jesus also showed zeal when confronting the Pharisees (Matt. 23), and Peter and John showed it when defying the Sanhedrin (Acts 4:20). Although servant leadership has a strong biblical foundation, it is missing the component of zeal that is often seen in biblical leaders. Therefore, I contend that Level 5 is the most biblical form of leadership, as well as successful in all types of organizations in the 21st century.

Intense Resolve

Intense resolve is probably the construct of indomitable will that most closely aligns with the term indomitable will. Resolve is defined as "firm determination to do something,"[48] and to do so intensely is to do it with "extreme force, degree, or strength."[49] In other words, the effort that is put into the task is not modest. It truly is "an absolute, obsessed, burning, compulsive ambition."[50]

There are numerous stories of great men and women who have had intense resolve for their faith or charitable cause, but perhaps the most interesting story from *Good to Great*[51] is that of businessman Darwin Smith of Kimberly-Clark Corporation. He was a humble and soft-spoken man who said at this retirement that he never stopped trying to be qualified for the job of CEO.[52] Collins says that "his lack of pretense was coupled with a fierce, even stoic,

47. "Dictionary by Merriam-Webster."
48. "Oxford Dictionary on Lexico.Com."
49. "Oxford Dictionary on Lexico.Com."
50. Collins, "From Good to Great: What Defines a Level V Leader?"
51. Collins, *Good to Great.*
52. Collins, "The Triumph of Humility and Fierce Resolve."

resolve toward life."[53] When he was surprisingly picked to become CEO of this paper company in 1971, the stock had dropped 40% in the past 20 years and the industry outlook was bleak. He led a stunning turnaround by selling the paper mills that were the core of the business and investing in developing consumer product brands such as Kleenex, Huggies, Kotex, Cottonelle, and Depends. He stated that "we will achieve greatness or perish."[54] Although the implementation of this strategy against incredible pressure from inside and outside the organization could adequately illustrate the intense resolve he possessed for the organization, the conditions under which he accomplished it were extraordinary. Two months after he became CEO, Smith was diagnosed with nose and throat cancer and given less than a year to live. He continued on the job, commuting from Wisconsin to Texas twice per week for radiation treatments, and was CEO for another 20 years until his retirement. "Smith's ferocious resolve was crucial to the rebuilding of Kimberly-Clark."[55]

In her book *Grit*, Angela Duckworth explores the importance of intense resolve that characterizes Level 5 leaders.[56] She emphasizes the importance of the rare characteristic of endurance and states that "as much as talent counts, effort counts twice."[57] Everyone suffers setbacks and failures, but success belongs to those who have the resolve to repeatedly pick themselves up and try again.

Dedication to the Organization

Dedication to the organization is best communicated through stories of dedicated individuals, and my family has been connected with a group of extraordinary individuals who were dedicated to an organization and a cause. In 1969, a 32-year-old professor

53. Collins, "The Triumph of Humility and Fierce Resolve."
54. "Darwin Smith."
55. Collins, "The Triumph of Humility and Fierce Resolve."
56. Duckworth, *Grit.*
57. Duckworth, *Grit.*

became the president of a 76-year-old Bible college that was struggling financially. The college was founded in the poverty-stricken post-civil war south and is "Open day and night to the poor young man who desires above every other desire to preach the Gospel of Christ."[58] His first step was to create a leadership team of five men who shared his philosophy of leadership and commitment to the college. The shortest tenure of any of those leaders in their positions ended up being 25 years, and that team of six men transformed the college from good to great. During the president's 38-year tenure enrollment quadrupled, the endowment multiplied, and the college has been listed as one of the most financially fit universities in America.[59] While many of its peer colleges and universities are struggling and failing, this one is thriving. I believe the difference is the dedication and commitment of the leadership to the organization and to its mission focused on the Great Commission (Matt. 18:28-30).

This is the story of Dr. David Eubanks, president of Johnson Bible College, now Johnson University. When Dr. Eubanks was developing his leadership team in 1970, leadership studies and publications had not yet defined his style. At that point in history, transformational leadership might have been the closest definition, but it was insufficient. In the 1970s and 1980s, Christian organizations gravitated to Robert Greenleaf's servant leadership model, but it fell short in describing what was happening at Johnson Bible College and other dynamic organizations. This leadership style was best described as Level 5 leadership. If Jim Collins conducted research that included higher education, I believe that he would have a picture of David Eubanks and his team as the embodiment of Level 5 leadership. The leadership team embodied that absolute, obsessed, burning, compulsive ambition for the mission of Johnson.

My father, Wilbur Reid Jr., was part of the leadership team that Dr. Eubanks established in 1970, and my mom is believed to be the longest tenured employee at Johnson with over 50 years of

58. Johnson, "Johnson: A History."

59. Coudriet, "Forbes' 2019 College Financial Health Grades."

service that were mostly spent as the secretary for my father and Dr. Eubanks. The long hours, effort, and dedication they put into the college have become legendary lore that began with the understanding that the job description of a leader is simply the starting point. For example, he went to the office one morning to prepare for visitors arriving later in the day, and he thought the front of the building did not look sharp, so he pressure-washed it in his suit and tie at 6:00 a.m. In another story, a member of the Senior Saints group visiting campus for the week called him at 2:00 a.m. because he couldn't sleep due to a soft mattress, so dad went down to the college shop in the middle of the night, cut a piece of plywood the size of the bed to make it firm, and tucked the guest in by 3:00 a.m. Stories like these could fill an entire book, but they should not be considered the stories of a workaholic or someone with personal ambition. He had a genuine passion for the cause so the work was a joy. He would rather be at the office doing something productive than at home watching TV. This attitude illustrates the obsessed dedication of a leader to the organization.

Throughout their tenure at Johnson, mom and dad were an inseparable team. When he died in 2013, several people said that "you can't say Wilbur without saying Linda." As teenagers, if my brother and I were away from home and wanted to find mom and dad at 9:00 p.m., we would call the office first because they were usually there together. We always had dinner together, and they never missed a ballgame or event that we participated in. Knowing they would be travelling a lot to represent the college, one of the conditions they stipulated upon taking the job was that the family would travel with him. The college bought a travel trailer so we would be together. In 2012, the trustees of Johnson established the Wilbur and Linda Reid Second Mile Award to honor a staff member each year who has a "servant heart and who is passionate about the university,"[60] which sounds just like Level 5 leadership. They demonstrated that it is possible to be intensely dedicated to the organization without neglecting other priorities.

---

60. "Wilbur, Linda Reid Second Mile Award Honors Lifestyle of Service."

This is just one story of the leadership team. Interestingly, the zeal of those six men on the leadership team for the ministry of Johnson influenced their children: 50 years after this leadership team was formed, each of those leaders has a son or daughter who is currently working at the university. As the son of one of those leaders who began at Johnson around 1970, I grew up literally living on campus, and I believed that all leaders were humble and had a passionate dedication to their cause. As I moved off campus as an adult, I realized the leadership that I had witnessed was a rare exception. When *Good to Great* was released,[61] I became fascinated with Level 5 leadership because it finally provided a framework that effectively described the rare leadership that I had witnessed growing up.

A Clear Catalyst in Achieving Results

In his various books, Collins has a lot to say about achieving successful results. In his first book, *Built to Last: Successful Habits of Visionary Companies*, Collins presents the idea of BHAGs, or Big Hairy Audacious Goals.[62] All organizations have goals, but a BHAG is a clear and compelling goal that requires great effort and a unified team spirit to accomplish. "A BHAG engages people. It reaches out and grabs them in the gut. It is tangible, energizing, highly focused. People 'get it' right away; it takes little or no explanation."[63] A famous example of a BHAG is from John Kennedy's speech to Congress in 1961: "I believe that this nation should commit itself to achieving the goal, before this decade is out, of landing a man on the moon and returning him safely to the earth. . . . We choose to go to the moon in this decade and do the other things. Not because they are easy, but because they are hard."[64] Churches and Christian nonprofits like to say that the goal is so big, if God is not

61. Collins, *Good to Great.*

62. Collins and Porras, *Built to Last.*

63. Collins and Porras, *Built to Last,* 94.

64. Hansen, "The 'Man on the Moon' Standard."

in it, it will fail. The Level 5 leader is a clear catalyst in achieving the results.

In his 2011 book *Great by Choice: Uncertainty, Chaos, and Luck*, Collins makes the case that luck, both good and bad, is often involved in outcomes of decisions made by leaders.[65] In fact, research has shown that leaders who make decisions that result in success are more likely to be considered lucky, while those who make decisions that result in failures tend to be considered poor decision makers.[66] Therefore, being a clear catalyst means the leader does not simply benefit from good luck but is actively involved in achieving the results.[67]

Strong Work Ethic

The Protestant work ethic, which has been a key component of the success of western economies, is based on the idea that every person has a vocation that is a calling from God. The correlation between hard work and success is self-evident. The Biblical foundation begins in the Old Testament from the wisdom of Solomon: "Whatever your hand finds to do, do it with all your might" (Eccl. 9:10) and "Those who work their land will have abundant food" (Prov 12:11). The apostle Paul says "Whatever you do, work at it with all your heart, as working for the Lord, not for human masters, since you know that you will receive an inheritance from the Lord as a reward. It is the Lord Christ you are serving" (Col. 3:23,24). N.T. Wright notes that the motivation for the work ethic is generated not from the importance of the work or external rewards, but from an internal desire to turn a job or a task into an act of worship.[68] Since the work is motivated by a desire to serve Jesus, it is not impacted by the amount or likelihood of a reward.[69]

---

65. Collins and Hansen, *Great by Choice.*
66. Erkal, Gangadharan, and Koh, "By Chance or By Choice?"
67. Collins, *Good to Great.*
68. Wright, Larsen, and Larsen, *Colossians and Philemon.*
69. Wright, Larsen, and Larsen.

Some people believe that a strong work ethic means working all the time. However, the Biblical practice of a sabbath (shabbat) and sabbatical is a critical concept for hard-working people to grasp.[70] Though long hours and hard work will likely yield short-term results, it will lead to burnout and damaged relationships that will be detrimental to the leader over the long-term. A sabbatical does not need to fit a pre-determined pattern and will likely look different for each leader. While a sabbath refers to one day per week with faith and family, a sabbatical is a period away from regular responsibilities. A sabbatical is not to be confused with an extended vacation. A sabbatical should be a planned, strategic job pause—paid or unpaid—whereby an individual takes time to disconnect from what is usual, to travel, do research, volunteer, learn a new skill, or fulfill a lifelong dream before returning to regular work.[71] Therefore, a strong work ethic must be combined with strategic time off.

Self-Motivated

Being a leader is hard. In addition to the requirement of time and energy, there are inevitable disappointments and heartbreaks. Being a follower is much easier. Whether one gradually grows into a leadership role or is suddenly thrust into a position of authority and expected to lead, growing into an effective leader requires characteristics and behaviors that seem to vary widely from one leader to another.

If there is one characteristic that all effective leaders seem to possess, it is motivation.[72] Some are motivated by external sources such as money or power, but Level 5 leaders are self-motivated to achieve. They have an internal drive that causes them to achieve beyond expectations, and they would do it regardless of compensation or threats. The difference between externally motivated and self-motivated people can be seen in their passion for what they

70. Reid, "A Sabbatical for Volunteers."
71. Reid, "A Sabbatical for Volunteers."
72. Goleman, *Emotional Intelligence.*

do. They are often restless with the status quo, and they love to learn, look for creative challenges, and take great satisfaction from the successful completion of a job or a goal attained.[73] They like to keep score, and they are continually raising the performance expectations within the organization.

The distinction between being self-motivated and externally motivated may be difficult to determine from a distance, but it is an important factor to identify. If a leader is motivated by money or power, their motivation to lead and the way they lead will likely change when those external factors change. However, if their motivation comes from who they are, they will remain a consistent and predictable leader regardless of the external forces that will be constantly changing. This is especially important in times of change or crisis.

A few years ago, I was leading a team of analysts at a Fortune 500 company. About half of our job was supporting our small business customers so they could be more profitable. I often travelled to meet our customers and work with them directly. I learned a lot about the people in these businesses, who were often literally Mom and Pop. When I returned to the office, I enjoyed telling stories about how the work of the analysts was helping the owners send their kids to college, provide wages for more employees, and support their churches and charities. The team indicated that helping other people elevated their motivation beyond a paycheck.

A simple story illustrates the concept of what motivates people. "Three bricklayers are asked: 'What are you doing?' The first says, 'I am laying bricks.' The second says, 'I am building a church.' And the third says, 'I am building the house of God.' The first bricklayer has a job. The second has a career. The third has a calling."[74]

---

73. Goleman, "What Makes a Leader? IQ And Technical Skills Are Important, but Emotional Intelligence Is the Sine qua Non of Leadership."

74. Duckworth, *Grit.*

21

Empirical Research

Boss Performance and Leadership Style

THE FIRST STUDY UTILIZING THE new L5LS examined the perceptions of employees regarding their bosses, which was first presented at the International Leadership Association (ILA) conference[1] and then published in a peer reviewed journal.[2] To establish credibility in the new instrument, this research utilized an instrument to measure servant leadership[3] and the well-established Multifactor Leadership Questionnaire (MLQ-5X) that measures the full range leadership model, which includes transformational, transactional and passive leadership types.[4]

This study investigates follower perceptions of bosses. The first perception examined is the relationship between performance results of the boss and three leadership types: transformational leadership, Level 5 leadership, and servant leadership. Extensive

1. Reid, "Service and Humility in Leadership: Intriguing Theories, but Do They Actually Produce Results?," 2016.

2. Wilbur Reid, "Service and Humility in Leadership: Intriguing Theories, but Do They Actually Produce Results?" *Servant Leadership: Theory and Practice* 4, no. 2 (2017): 27–52.

3. Winston and Fields, "Seeking and Measuring the Essential Behaviors of Servant Leadership."

4. Bass and Avolio, "Multifactor Leadership Questionnaire."

research has shown a consistent positive relationship between transformational leadership and performance results, but there is a dearth of empirical research on servant and Level 5 leadership. Surveys were completed by 267 employees, or followers, that resulted in scores for transformational leadership, servant leadership, and Level 5 leadership, as well as the followers' perception of boss performance results. The data show that all three leadership types were statistically significant in predicting boss performance results. Although Level 5, servant leadership, and transformational leadership are different constructs and are theoretically different, there was a strong and statistically significant correlation in the followers' perception of each of these leadership types. Based on follower perception, they are statistically similar. Their relationship to perceived boss performance results is important because it contradicts the idea that servant leaders are simply doormats that are taken advantage of and can't be effective leaders. On the contrary, these leaders who serve their followers account for the most variability in the followers' perception of boss success.

Courage, Religious Commitment, and Humble Leadership

Is there a statistically significant relationship between the leader's perception of his or her courage, servant leadership, Level 5 leadership, and religious commitment? In this study. instead of asking participants to rate other leaders, they were asked to rate themselves on Level 5 leadership, servant leadership, religious commitment, and courage.[5] Moderating variables include gender, race, and generation. Key findings from self-reported data of 465 participants:

- The following variables are positively and statistically significant correlated:

---

5. Reid, "The Impact of Religious Commitment on Servant and Level 5 Leadership."

- o Level 5 leaders are statistically the same people as servant leaders, even though the constructs are different.

- o Level 5 and servant leaders develop other leaders.

- o Level 5 and servant leaders have a higher level of religious commitment than other leaders.

- o Level 5 and servant leaders are more courageous than other leaders.

- o Level 5 and servant leaders are older than other leaders.

- o Level 5 leaders and servant leaders are more educated than non-Level 5 leaders.

- Other conclusions
  - o There is no statistically significant difference in fear within leadership types, but servant and Level 5 leaders overcome their fear (courage).

  - o Gender is not a relevant variable in leadership, but women are more likely to admit fear, and men are more likely to claim courage.

Service and Humility in Crisis Leadership

With the data from research showing that Level 5 is an effective style of leadership, another study was completed to evaluate how Level 5 and servant leadership performed in times of crisis or turbulent times.[6] In times of crisis, people turn to leaders for guidance and inspiration. Literature theorizes that servant leaders might be particularly effective in times of crisis: "Ego works in the face of genuine crisis,"[7] indicating that the subjugation of the ego into service to followers is more effective in navigating crisis. However, there had not yet been any published empirical evidence

6. Reid, "Service & Humility in Crisis Leadership: Intriguing Theories, but Do They Actually Produce Results?"; Reid, *Service & Humility in Crisis Leadership*.

7. Greenleaf, *Servant Leadership*, 6.

to support that theory. The purpose of this research was to identify the leaders that people turn to in crisis and then ascertain the type and effectiveness of that leadership. Utilizing the definition of a leader as anyone who influences the thoughts and behaviors of others,[8] this leader could be one with formal authority or one with no formal authority. Participants were asked to identify the person they turned to in a specific time of crisis. They were then asked to evaluate the effectiveness of that leader during the time of crisis. Finally, they assessed the servant leadership and Level 5 leadership behaviors exhibited by each of the leaders. Servant leadership was measured utilizing the ten-item Essential Servant Leader Behaviors instrument from Winston and Fields,[9] and Level 5 leadership was measured utilizing the ten-item Level 5 Leadership Scale.[10]

An analysis of the data shows that each of these leadership types is effective in crisis, but that Level 5 leadership has the strongest relationship with success. Higher ranked leaders have more success in bringing an organization out of crisis. Leaders who score higher in servant leadership have more success in bringing organizations out of crisis. Finally, Level 5 leaders have more success.

8. Sims, *Managing Organizational Behavior*, 221.

9. Winston and Fields, "Seeking and Measuring the Essential Behaviors of Servant Leadership."

10. Reid, "Development of an Instrument to Measure Level 5 Leadership."

22

Servant Leadership

SERVANT LEADERSHIP IS A PECULIAR TERM. The two words almost seem mutually exclusive. You can either be a servant or a leader, but not at the same time. It is a paradoxical idea that is difficult to grasp. However, research is demonstrating that servant leadership not only leads to financial success, but also improves the important organizational goals of ethical business practices and global competitiveness.[1]

Although the concepts of servant leadership are ancient, the modern theory and practice of servant leadership began with Robert Greenleaf in the 1970s.[2] Greenleaf is the undisputed father of modern servant leadership, and he observed that the focus of servant leadership is on the development and performance of the follower.[3] He described the motivation behind the desire to lead:

> The servant-leader is servant first . . . It begins with the natural feeling that one wants to serve first. Then

---

1. Kiker, Scully Callahan, and Kiker, "Exploring the Boundaries of Servant Leadership: A Meta-Analysis of the Main and Moderating Effects of Servant Leadership on Behavioral and Affective Outcomes."

2. Greenleaf, *Servant Leadership*; Greenleaf, "The Servant as Leader (an Essay)."

3. Winston and Fields, "Seeking and Measuring the Essential Behaviors of Servant Leadership."

conscious choice brings one to aspire to lead. That person is sharply different from one who is leader first, perhaps because of the need to assuage an unusual power drive or to acquire material possessions. For such it will be a later choice to serve—after leadership is established. The leader-first and the servant-first are two extreme types ... The difference manifests itself in the care taken by the servant-first to make sure that other people's highest priority needs are being served.[4]

Following the introduction of servant leadership into modern leadership research by Greenleaf, studies have sought to define measures to quantify the attributes of a servant leader.[5] Perhaps the greatest challenge in the study of servant leadership is that Greenleaf was somewhat vague about the definition of servant leadership, so there is a wide range of definitions and theories and no clear consensus of what servant leadership is.[6] In the book *Servant Leadership in Action*, which I enthusiastically recommend, Ken Blanchard and Renee Broadwell compiled 42 essays on servant leadership from current leaders and experts on the topic.[7] While full of wonderful content, it becomes clear that everyone seems to have their own understanding of servant leadership.

Two key studies in 2015 sought to resolve this issue by examining the wide range of literature and experts on the topic, focusing on the past 40 years, to determine if a consensus could be reached. The first study was completed by Winston and Fields, who were two of my Ph.D. professors, with Winston being the chair of my dissertation committee. They examined the extensive literature on

4. Greenleaf, *Servant Leadership*, 13.

5. Dennis and Bocarnea, "Servant Leadership Assessment Instrument"; Patterson, Redmer, and Stone, "Transformational Leaders to Servant Leaders versus Level 4 Leaders to Level 5 Leaders - The Move from Good to Great"; Winston and Fields, "Seeking and Measuring the Essential Behaviors of Servant Leadership."

6. Bryant and Brown, "Getting to Know the Elephant"; Focht and Ponton, "Identifying Primary Characteristics of Servant Leadership."

7. Blanchard and Broadwell, *Servant Leadership in Action. How You Can Achieve Great Relationships and Results.*

servant leadership, and they identified and validated "ten leader behaviors that seem to be essential to servant leadership."[8] These behaviors are:

- Practices what he or she preaches;

- Serves people without regard to their nationality, gender, or race;

- Sees serving as a mission of responsibility to others;

- Shows genuinely interested in employees as people;

- Understands that serving others is most important;

- Is willing to make sacrifices to help others;

- Seeks to instill trust rather than fear or insecurity;

- Is always honest;

- Is driven by a sense of higher calling; and

- Promotes values that transcend self-interest and material success.[9]

The data were validated so this research could be used as an instrument to measure servant leadership. These behaviors have been used to establish a relationship with Level 5 leadership.[10]

The second notable study that sought to bring consensus to the definition of servant leadership was by Focht and Ponton.[11] There are three key differences in this study. First, Focht and Ponton focused on the *characteristics* of the leaders instead of their

8. Winston and Fields, "Seeking and Measuring the Essential Behaviors of Servant Leadership."

9. Winston and Fields, "Seeking and Measuring," 424.

10. Reid, "Service and Humility in Leadership: Intriguing Theories, but Do They Actually Produce Results?," 2016; Reid, *Service & Humility in Crisis Leadership*; Reid, "Service & Humility in Crisis Leadership: Intriguing Theories, but Do They Actually Produce Results?"; Reid, "The Impact of Religious Commitment on Servant and Level 5 Leadership"; Reid, "Service and Humility in Leadership: Intriguing Theories, but Do They Actually Produce Results?," 2017.

11. Focht and Ponton, "Identifying Primary Characteristics of Servant Leadership."

behaviors. Second, they did not validate it for use as an instrument to measure servant leadership. Third, instead of examining the extant literature, they gathered an expert panel of authors of peer-reviewed journal articles on the topic of servant leadership into a Delphi study, which utilizes multiple rounds of questionnaires to arrive at a consensus. After the third and final round, the experts determined there are 12 primary characteristics that are essential to servant leadership:

- Value people
- Humility
- Listening
- Trust
- Caring
- Integrity
- Service
- Empowering
- Serve others' needs before their own
- Collaboration
- Love, unconditional love
- Learning.[12]

These characteristics will be explored further in the next chapter.

As the millennial generation is entering the workforce, the discussion of servant leadership in corporate America is escalating. Organizations are moving away from traditional, hierarchical, patriarchal, and top-down structures where employees serve their bosses. Today, servant leadership is a more effective model for employee-centric organizations that foster innovation, engagement, and employee well-being.[13] Christians are particularly interested

---

12. Focht and Ponton, "Identifying Primary Characteristics."

13. Eva, Sendjaya, Prajogo, Cavanagh, and Robin, "Creating Strategic Fit"; Khan, Mubarik, and Islam, "Leading the Innovation."

in promoting servant leadership because it is consistent with the teachings of Jesus and his disciples (John 13:12-16, Mark 10:42-45, 1 Peter 5:1-14, Philippians 2:1-5).

Since 1998, *Fortune* magazine has published the annual *Fortune* 100 Best Companies to work for, which is compiled by Michael Bush and his organization Great Place to Work.[14] Their work encompasses surveys of over 10 million employees and 50 countries annually and found that companies that are great places to work outperform their peers in all of the key metrics, including profitability, sales growth, and stock performance. They also found a significant correlation between being a great place to work and leaders who exhibit servant leader characteristics, whether they call it servant leadership or not.[15] Most of the companies they work with are secular by nature, but "the leaders of companies building great places to work act in keeping with the great faith traditions, regardless of personal religion or spiritual beliefs. They demonstrate humility, elevate the least powerful, and treat all people with dignity."[16]

Although there are some high-profile corporations such as Chick-Fil-A, Nordstrom, SAS, and Southwest Airlines that have been very successful utilizing servant leadership, there is more than just anecdotal evidence finding servant leadership produces results. A meta-analysis of 67 studies of servant leadership found the following:

- Servant leadership leads to positive outcomes for both the individual and the organization.

- Servant leadership had a positive effect on the job performance, trust, organizational commitment, and attitudes of employees.

- Interestingly, servant leadership showed higher results in individualistic cultures than collectivist cultures.

---

14. Bush, "Servant Leaders Create a Great Place to Work."
15. Bush, "Servant Leaders Create a Great Place to Work."
16. Bush, "Servant Leaders Create a Great Place to Work."

- Although results of servant leadership were positive in all settings, results were higher in non-business settings than in business settings.

- Men respond to servant leadership primarily indicated by higher job performance, while women respond more attitudinally through higher job satisfaction, commitment, and trust.[17]

Servant leadership literature consists primarily of conceptual work, especially in terms of characteristics, measurement development, and theoretical framework development.[18] There has been very little development of incremental servant leadership theory in recent years.

Toward the end of a ministry spent serving the common man with teaching and healing, John records two occasions when Jesus was with his disciples and modeled servant leadership. The first was in the upper room at the last supper when Jesus demonstrated servant leadership by washing his disciples' feet and then instructing them to do likewise (John 13:14). After his resurrection, Jesus invited the disciples to breakfast on the shore and once again demonstrated servant leadership by preparing breakfast and serving it to them (John 21:12, 13). The life of Jesus exemplified the nature of being a servant. Servant leaders establish trust "by being completely honest and open, keeping actions consistent with values, and showing trust in followers."[19] The leadership that Jesus modeled for the disciples was revolutionary for his time, but his disciples learned from him, and this small group of men changed the world by implementing servant leadership in churches (1 Peter 5:1-6).

When Peter denied that he knew Jesus three times, his relationship with Jesus may have been irreparably damaged, as Judas'

17. Kiker, Scully Callahan, and Kiker, "Exploring the Boundaries of Servant Leadership: A Meta-Analysis of the Main and Moderating Effects of Servant Leadership on Behavioral and Affective Outcomes."

18. Parris and Peachey, "A Systematic Literature Review of Servant Leadership Theory in Organizational Contexts."

19. Greenleaf, *Servant Leadership*.

relationship with Jesus was destroyed (Matt 27:3-5). However, Peter desired to restore the relationship, and Jesus used the opportunity on the lakeshore after the resurrection to transform Peter's life (John 21). Peter's loyalty to Jesus changed the world. The transformation in Peter's life can be seen in other New Testament texts. Peter is the one who led the preaching on the first day of the church on the day of Pentecost, which resulted in three thousand baptisms (Acts 2). He healed the sick (Acts 3:1-10), provided leadership for the church (Acts 15, 1 Peter, 2 Peter), and boldly spoke about Jesus wherever he went (Acts 3:11-26, 4:1-22, 8:14-25, 10).

Jesus related to his followers, had compassion for them, and served them. He appealed to them not only to act appropriately, but also to look to the inside to transform their way of thinking. Paul summarized it in this philosophy: "Do not conform to the pattern of this world but be transformed by the renewing of your mind. Then you will be able to test and approve what God's will is—his good, pleasing and perfect will" (Rom. 12:2). In contrast, the Pharisees focused on external actions, were out of touch with their followers, and generally practiced transactional leadership.[20]

While servant leadership is about serving, it should never be confused with weakness or being subservient. Servant leaders are powerful,[21] and the foundation of servant leadership is courage.[22] However, that power and courage is invested in relationships. One reason courage is foundational is that leaders, including servant leaders, must find their voices.[23] Aspiring leaders listen to mentors, read books, and go to conferences to learn as much as possible from others, and that learning never stops. However, the turning point for you as a leader comes when you find your own voice. You realize that you don't need position, title, talent, techniques, or someone else's words, because you have found your true voice

---

20. Robinson, "Leadership That Matters."

21. Ramsey, "Leading Is Serving."

22. Brown, "In the Service of Others."

23. Kouzes and Posner, "Finding Your Voice."

that was developed through your life experiences, and you have summoned the courage to step out and use it.[24]

24. Kouzes and Posner, "Finding Your Voice."

23

Characteristics of Servant Leaders

Since Focht and Ponton[1] developed a consensus with the experts of servant leadership to identify the characteristics of servant leaders and the definitions of those characteristics, it is appropriate to utilize their definitions to examine the 12 characteristics.

Value people

Servant leaders truly value people for who they are, not just for what they give to the organization. Servant leaders are first and foremost committed to people, particularly their followers.

Humility

Servant leaders do not promote themselves; they promote others . . . putting others first. They are truly humble, not humble as an act. Servant leaders understand it is not about them—things happen through others. Exemplary servant leaders know they cannot do it alone.

---

1. Focht and Ponton, "Identifying Primary Characteristics of Servant Leadership."

Listening

Listens receptively—nonjudgmentally. They are willing to listen because they truly want to learn from others. To understand follower/associates, they must listen deeply, and they seek first to understand. Discernment enables one to know when or where service is needed.

Trust

Servant leaders give trust to others. They are willing to take risks to serve others well. Servant leaders are trusted because they are authentic and dependable.

Caring

Servant leaders truly have the people and the purpose in their heart. They display a kindness toward others and a concern for others. As the term implies, they are there to serve others and not to be served by others. Servant leaders care more for the people than for the organization.

Integrity

Servant leaders are honest, credible, and can be trusted. They do not cut corners. They allow dependability and trust—something you can count on. Integrity is knowing what your values are, developing a set of shared values with the people you serve, and then remaining true to those values. This provides clarity and drives commitment. Servant leaders need to be first in ensuring that their behaviors are consistent with their values and with the shared values they develop with others. This includes the categories of engaging in honest self-evaluation, inner consciousness, and spirituality.

Service

The servant leader is servant first.

Empowering

Servant leaders empower others and expect accountability.

Serve others' needs before their own

Servant leaders serve others before self. This is foundational to what it means to be a servant leader. Put others' interests before our own.

Collaboration

Servant leaders reject the need for competition and pitting people against each other. They bring people together. Because servant leadership is about pursuing a higher purpose for the good of the whole and because leadership is by definition a collaborative process (it requires collaboration between leaders and followers), skilled collaboration is an essential characteristic of a servant leader. This includes categories of accountability, awareness, building community, courage in relationships, empathy, and listening. Servant leaders do not go it alone; they work together with others in collaborative endeavors that serve the needs of followers and their organization.

Love, unconditional love

Unconditional love is a strong phrase with Christian overtones, so it might be better to call it something else, such as acceptance or appreciation, but it is a radical and powerful starting point for servant leadership because it becomes the primary motivator for the way you treat other people. If you start with a posture of unconditional love (believing that every person is as worthy and valuable as you are and committing to dealing with them in the most loving way possible in every circumstance), it transforms how you treat them and how you understand your higher purpose. This category includes acceptance, acknowledging, appreciation of others, equality, trust, and vulnerability. The ultimate motive to serve.

Learning

This includes learning from those below them in the organization. Servant leaders are learners. They truly want to learn from others. They know that they do not know it all, so they are willing to learn from all directions in the organization. Great leaders never rest when it comes to learning about future trends and opportunities, the perspectives of their multiple internal and external stakeholders, the emergence of new ideas and technologies related to their business, and the art and science of leadership itself. Learning is the master skill that leads to growth, including personally, relationally, organizationally, and in broader society. This includes comfort with ambiguity and intellectual energy and curiosity.[2]

---

2. Focht and Ponton, "Identifying Primary Characteristics of Servant Leadership."

24

Comparing Level 5
and Servant Leadership

ALTHOUGH LEVEL 5 AND SERVANT leadership have unique constructs, the differences may not be discernable to followers.[1] A common perception among business leaders is that Level 5 leadership is just another name for servant leadership.[2] Additionally, in academia, it has been suggested that Level 5 leadership may be the same as servant leadership,[3] that servant leaders are more likely to be Level 5 leaders,[4] that there is a clear overlap between Level 5 and servant leadership,[5] and that "there are marked similarities between the behavior of those termed Level 5 leaders and the servant or humble leader."[6] In the development of a validated instrument

1. Stone, Russell, and Patterson, "Transformational versus Servant Leadership: A Difference in Leader Focus."

2. Lichtenwalner, "Servant Leadership Lesson."

3. Patterson, Redmer, and Stone, "Transformational Leaders to Servant Leaders versus Level 4 Leaders to Level 5 Leaders - The Move from Good to Great"; Drury, "Employee Perceptions of Servant Leadership: Comparisons by Level with Job Satisfaction and Organizational Commitment."

4. Wong and Davey, "Best Practices in Servant Leadership"; Reid, "Service and Humility in Leadership: Intriguing Theories, but Do They Actually Produce Results?," 2017.

5. van Dierendonck, "Servant Leadership."

6. Morris, Brotheridge, and Urbanski, "Bringing Humility to Leadership,"

to measure Level 5 leadership, I found there was no statistically significant difference between leaders who were identified as Level 5 leaders and servant leaders.[7] In fact, corporations like the term servant leadership, but may be using a style that is closer to Level 5 leadership. For example, Southwest Airlines is a long-time outspoken proponent of servant leadership and describe their three key values as "warrior spirit, servant heart, and fun-LUVing attitude."[8]

If the research is telling us that Level 5 leaders and servant leaders are usually the same people, then why are there two different constructs? There are two key distinctions: focus of the leader and indomitable will. In servant leadership, the focus of the leader is on serving the followers. If the organization benefits, then that it is a happy bonus. Alternatively, a Level 5 leader is intensely focused on the success of the organization. If the follower benefits, then that it is a happy bonus. When a Level 5 leader has put aside his personal pride for the good of organization, he usually recognizes that serving the followers is the best path for organizational success.

While there is a strong link between servant leadership and the humility component of Level 5 leadership, servant leadership does not incorporate the indomitable will, or zeal, of Level 5 leadership. The servant leader does not necessarily have the "absolute, obsessed, burning, compulsive ambition"[9] of the Level 5 leader. For example, I have seen sales managers of large corporations who were servant leaders for their sales reps but did not have a passion for their work and had little interest in the success of the corporation. There are pastors who are content to serve the people in their churches and communities, but do not have the energy or enthusiasm to accomplish much.

Although servant leadership is by far the most popular leadership theory among Christians, I believe that Level 5 leadership is the most closely aligned with Christian leadership taught and

---

1323.

7. Reid, "Development of an Instrument to Measure Level 5 Leadership."

8. Barrett, "Treat Your People as Family," 185.

9. Collins, "From Good to Great: What Defines a Level V Leader?"

demonstrated in the Bible. Using a church setting to examine the focus of the Christian leader, everyone would agree that serving the followers in the congregation and accomplishing the mission of the church are both desirable goals and usually not mutually exclusive. However, when there is a conflict and a choice must be made between doing what is best for a follower being served or the mission of the church, where does your loyalty lie? This question is relevant in any type of organization. If a business focuses on serving employees to the detriment of other necessary functions and goes into bankruptcy, there will be no employees to serve. Therefore, loyalties must start with the cause or the mission first, and then with serving the followers.[10] In addition to the focus and loyalty of the leaders, the evidence of zeal and passion in leaders, as described in the chapter about the characteristics of Level 5 leadership, is evident throughout scripture and is a component that is not adequately addressed in servant leadership. Therefore, while Level 5 and servant are both desirable leadership types, if a distinction must be made, I find that the argument for Level 5 leadership in Christian leaders to be more compelling.

10. Catalyst, *Andy Stanley and Jim Collins.*

25

Gender in Servant and Level 5 Leadership

LEADERSHIP THEORY AND RESEARCH OVER the past 100 years has focused on the leaders of western culture, which are predominantly white males. This has led to a cognitive dissonance between women and traditional leadership styles that rely on the power of the position of the leader.[1] In general, whether leading or following, men are more comfortable with strong positional managerial leadership, while women prefer to lead and be led by a servant leadership style that is generally seen as a soft and caring role.[2] The following table summarizes research that shows the characteristics and skills that men and women tend to excel in[3]:

Men excel in these characteristics	Women excel in these characteristics
Tradition: build knowledge based on past experience	People skills: sensitivity, kind, listening, relationships
Innovation: open to new ideas and willing to take chances	Communication: make sure that their employees are well informed

1. Hogue, "Gender Bias in Communal Leadership."
2. Hogue, "Gender Bias in Communal Leadership."
3. Radu, Deaconu, and Frăsineanu, "Leadership and Gender Differences."

Strategy: sees the big picture	Feedback: update their team in terms of performance
Being calm: keep emotions in check	Aspirations: set high goals
Delegating: assign objectives and responsibilities	Empathy: strong connections with their team
Cooperation: good teammates	Motivation: energetic and enthusiastic
Persuasion (sell ideas and win people over)	

Masculine and feminine characteristics and skills are complementary in leadership, with neither being exclusively more desirable than the other.[4] Servant leadership incorporates qualities that are more often considered to be feminine qualities such as caring, interest in followers as people, and seeing serving as a mission of responsibility to others.[5]

The challenge that women aspiring to lead face is the conflicting role expectations of being a leader and being a female. In a traditional authoritarian or positional leadership position, they may act like a leader and be disliked as a woman, or act like a woman and be perceived as an incompetent leader.[6] They find it challenging to win in that traditional environment.

In addition to general cultural shifts related to gender equality, leadership trends are shifting towards more women in leadership, especially among millennials. Servant leadership matches the preferences and expectations of millennials more than positional leadership types.[7] In fact, women are more likely to choose servant leadership as their style of leadership and more likely to develop their followers into servant leaders.[8]

4. Radu, Deaconu, and Frăsineanu, "Leadership and Gender Differences."

5. Winston and Fields, "Seeking and Measuring the Essential Behaviors of Servant Leadership."

6. Hogue, "Gender Bias in Communal Leadership."

7. Nordbye and Irving, "Servant Leadership and Organizational Effectiveness: Examining Leadership Culture among Millennials within a US National Campus Ministry."

8. Lemoine and Blum, "Servant Leadership, Leader Gender, and Team

Leadership is moving away from positional-style leadership to more of a focus on influence that relies on a follower-centric approach which emphasizes care and respect.[9] "Various papers published on this topic develop and compare the feminine leadership with the masculine leadership. The feminine leadership style was called social-expressive, with personal attention paid to subordinates and with focus on a good work environment; by contrast, the masculine leadership style was described as an instrumental one, focused on giving directions."[10] This shift has brought servant leadership to the fore in the past ten years, and "has the potential to unlock leadership opportunities for women to lead effectively while maintaining a feminine style, empowering women leaders to inhabit both leader and gender roles authentically."[11] Since perceived inconsistencies in the leader role and the female gender role are diminished in servant leadership, organizational cultures built on servant leadership should see women better represented in leadership roles.

Level 5 leadership seems to be gender neutral, embodying the strengths of feminine qualities that are more prevalent in personal humility and the more masculine qualities that are embodied in indomitable will. Research shows that Level 5 is gender neutral, with no statistically significant difference in the measurement of Level 5 leaders.[12] Men and women are equally likely to display the paradoxical blend of personal humility and indomitable will.

Gender Role."

9. Lehrke and Sowden, "Servant Leadership and Gender."

10. Radu, Deaconu, and Frăsineanu, "Leadership and Gender Differences—Are Men and Women Leading in the Same Way?"

11. Lehrke and Sowden, "Servant Leadership and Gender," 26.

12. Reid, "Development of an Instrument to Measure Level 5 Leadership."

26

Transformational Leadership

Overview of Transformational Leadership

Modern leadership research has been dominated by transformational leadership, comprising as much empirical research as all other types combined.[1] The research into the various leadership types have shown that transformational, authentic, servant, and Level 5 leaders are usually the same people, validated with statistical significance.[2] However, each has unique constructs and areas of focus.

Authentic leadership theory focuses on the attributes of the leader. All transformational leaders are authentic, but not all authentic leaders are transformational.[3] For example, an authentic leader may have a positive impact on his followers as a result of his example, but he may not be doing anything that actively develops his followers into leaders. Transformational leadership theory helps to collect the pieces of the puzzle that compose leadership in

1. Banks, McCauley, Gardner, and Guler, "A Meta-Analytic Review of Authentic and Transformational Leadership: A Test for Redundancy."

2. Banks, McCauley, Gardner, and Guler, "A Meta-Analytic Review of Authentic and Transformational Leadership: A Test for Redundancy"; Reid, "Service and Humility in Leadership: Intriguing Theories, but Do They Actually Produce Results?," 2017.

3. Avolio and Gardner, "Authentic Leadership Development."

an effort to advance toward the picture that appears on the puzzle box. The examples of Biblical leaders and historical church leaders show that successful Christian leaders who transform lives and transform the world will be authentic, will relate well with followers, will nurture leaders, and will point followers to Christ.

Transformational, transactional, and passive-avoidant leadership remain popular topics of study.[4] Most relationships between leaders and followers, especially between supervisors and employers, are transactional in nature.[5] For example, an employee agrees to perform a certain task within the prescribed guidelines, and his employer agrees to compensate him for the work. An alternate approach to leadership is transformational leadership, which seeks to raise the consciousness of people above their own self-interests by appealing to higher ideals.[6] "Superior leadership performance — transformational leadership — occurs when leaders broaden and elevate the interests of their employees, when they generate awareness and acceptance of the purposes and mission of the group, and when they stir their employees to look beyond their own self-interest for the good of the group."[7] Great leaders strive for this more effective transformational leadership.

Avolio and Bass[8] developed the *full range leadership model* that addressed perceived short-comings of previous leadership models that do not account for all of the leadership characteristics. This model begins with identifying three broad types of leadership: (a) transformational, (b) transactional, and (c) passive / avoidant (laissez-faire). Passive individuals avoid engaging in leadership behaviors and are the least effective leaders. Transactional leaders focus on errors and exceptions, exchanging rewards for effort

---

4. Yammarino, Spangler, and Bass, "Transformational Leadership and Performance: A Longitudinal Investigation"; Northouse, *Leadership*; Arrington, "Lead with a Human Focus; for Christ's Sake!"

5. Bass, "From Transactional to Transformational Leadership: Learning to Share the Vision."

6. Burns, *Leadership*.

7. Bass, "From Transactional to Transformational Leadership: Learning to Share the Vision," 21.

8. Avolio and Bass, "MLQ: Self Evaluation Report."

and results and can be effective leaders. The most effective type of leadership is transformational because followers are inspired, challenged, and stimulated to pursue a vision.[9] Table 1 summarizes the difference between transactional and transformational leadership.[10]

Table 1

Transactional Leadership	Transformational Leadership
Recognize what their associates want to get from their work and try to see that they get it if their performance so warrants.	Raise associates' level of awareness of the importance of achieving valued outcomes and strategies for reaching them.
Exchange rewards and promises of reward for appropriate level of support.	Encourage associates to transcend their self-interest for the sake of the team, organization, or larger policy.
Respond to the needs and desires of associates as long as they are getting the job done.	Develop associates' needs to higher levels in such areas as achievement, autonomy, and affiliation, which can be both work-related and not work-related.

Note: **Adapted from *Leadership and Performance Beyond Expectations,* by B. Bass, 1985, New York: The Free Press**

9. Avolio and Bass, "MLQ: Self Evaluation Report."

10. Bass, *Leadership and Performance beyond Expectations.*

These three broad types of leadership contain sub-types of leadership that are called *full range leadership model factors* and are summarized in table 2.[11]

Table 2

Leadership Type	Full Range Leadership Model Factor Labels	Abbreviation
Transformational Leadership	Idealized Attributes	IA
	Idealized Behaviors	IB
The 5 I's of transformational leadership	Inspirational Motivation	IM
	Intellectual Stimulation	IS
	Individualized Consideration	IC
Transactional Leadership	Contingent Reward	CR
	Management-by-Exception: Active	MBEA
Passive-Avoidant Leadership Behaviors	Management-by-Exception: Passive	MBEP
	Laissez Faire	LF

Note: Adapted from *Multifactor Leadership Questionnaire: Manual and Sampler Set* by Avolio and Bass (2004)

A transformational leader is proactive and seeks to optimize performance by leading individuals to achieve higher results. The five factors within transformational leadership that describe how that happens are all labeled with words beginning with the letter "I," so they are called the *five I's of transformational leadership.* Idealized Attributes (IA) seek to determine if the leader is able to instill a certain way of thinking within the followers, such as a sense of pride, respect, and interest in others. Idealized Behavior (IB) is

11. Bass and Bass, *The Bass Handbook of Leadership: Theory, Research, and Managerial Applications*; Avolio and Bass, *Multifactor Leadership Questionnaire. Manual and Sampler Set*; Bass and Avolio, "Multifactor Leadership Questionnaire."

more action oriented and searches for behaviors such as talking about the values of the group, considering moral implications of decisions, and having a collective sense of mission. Inspirational Motivation (IM) captures enthusiasm, optimism, and confidence that goals will be achieved. Intellectual Stimulation (IS) is about seeking different perspectives to solve problems and suggesting new ways of doing things. Individual Consideration (IC) is about spending time with others in teaching and coaching and valuing the input of others in the group.[12]

Transactional leaders utilize rewards and punishment to lead followers to a desired outcome. Transactional leadership may take the form of Contingent Reward (CR) or Management-by-Exception: Active (MBEA). Contingent Reward utilizes specific goals and objectives and provides incentives to reward followers for obtaining those objectives. Management-by-Exception: Active focuses on exceptions and mistakes and directs attention toward failures so that standards can be met.[13] Passive—Avoidant Behavior is reactive and ineffective and can be divided into two types. Management-by-Exception: Passive (MBEP) waits until there is a problem and then responds to it. Laissez-Faire (LF) represents a vacuum of leadership and is not responsive at all.[14]

Research since the 1980s has shown that transformational leadership consistently leads to positive outcomes, transactional leadership has mixed results, and passive leadership consistently produces the worst outcomes.[15]

Understanding the mind of the transformational leader can be accomplished by examining some of the great transformational

---

12. Avolio and Bass, "MLQ: Self Evaluation Report."

13. Avolio and Bass, "MLQ: Self Evaluation Report."

14. Avolio and Bass, "MLQ: Self Evaluation Report."

15. Howell and Avolio, "Transformational Leadership, Transactional Leadership, Locus of Control, and Support for Innovation: Key Predictors of Consolidated-Business-Unit Performance"; Slvanathan and Fekken, "Emotional Intelligence, Moral Reasoning, and Transformational Leadership"; Bennett, "A Study of the Management Leadership Style Preferred by IT Subordinates"; Muller and Turner, "Matching the Project Manager's Leadership Style to Project Type."

leaders in the Bible and in church history. These transformational leaders are able to relate to their followers personally, and they motivate their followers to strive for a mission or purpose that is greater than them.

Leaders in the Bible

Transactional leaders appeal to followers' self-interests, while transformational leaders appeal to their moral values.[16] The Bible contains stories of both transactional and transformational leaders. Moses is recognized as one of the greatest leaders of history, but his leadership tended to be transactional. The Israelites did not accept him as a leader (Exod. 5:21, 6:9) until after nine plagues they realized he might be able to emancipate them from slavery. If things were going well, they followed Moses. However, they rejected his leadership when he was not giving them what they wanted. This rebellion was seen when Moses was receiving the Ten Commandments (Exod. 32:1), when the people were hungry (Exod. 16:2-12), thirsty (Exod. 17:1-6), threatened (Exod. 14:11), or did not want to fight (Num 14:1-4). Moses responded in a transactional manner: he provided manna, quail, water, or whatever appealed to their self-interests.

Joshua was the protégé of Moses and assumed leadership upon the death of Moses, but he appealed to the Israelites' moral values. At the end of his life, he told the people to choose who they would serve and had them swear that they would follow Yahweh forever (Josh. 24:14-24).

> Joshua gathered all the tribes of Israel to Shechem and summoned the elders, the heads, the judges, and the officers of Israel. And they presented themselves before God . . . "Now therefore fear the LORD and serve him in sincerity and in faithfulness. Put away the gods that your fathers served beyond the River and in Egypt and serve the LORD. And if it is evil in your eyes to serve the

16. Burns, *Leadership*; Bass and Bass, *The Bass Handbook of Leadership: Theory, Research, and Managerial Applications*.

LORD, choose this day whom you will serve, whether the gods your fathers served in the region beyond the River, or the gods of the Amorites in whose land you dwell. But as for me and my house, we will serve the LORD." (Josh. 24:1, 14-15).

Joshua's goal was to change the lives of the descendants of his followers in the Promised Land.

Perhaps the most remarkable difference between Moses and Joshua are their relationships with God and with their followers. Moses had a remarkable personal relationship with God, but constantly struggled in a combative relationship with his followers. Joshua did not seem to have the personal relationship with God that Moses did but had a much more positive relationship with the children of Israel so that they followed him and followed God more than they did under Moses. The Talmud says that Moses is like the sun and Joshua is like the moon.[17]

Moses was like the sun because he was close to God, and his radiance was sometimes so bright that the people could not even look at his face (Exod. 34:29-35). God spoke to him face to face (Num. 12:8), but his followers had difficulty speaking to him. "Moses' unparalleled awe of God was so great he simply could not fathom why his people did not trust God also. Ironically then, Moses' incomparable faith may have been precisely at the root of his struggles in leading the Israelites."[18] His struggles in leading the people began while they were still in Egypt, and the elders required miraculous signs before they believed God had sent him (Exod. 4:29-31), and then the people complained against Moses and Aaron throughout their lifetime (Exod. 5:20, 21; 15:24; 16:2,3; 17:2,3; Num. 14:2-4; 16:41; 20:2-5; 21:4-6; Deut. 1:12, 26-28). For example, in the wilderness, "the whole congregation of the people of Israel grumbled against Moses and Aaron, and the people of Israel said to them, 'Would that we had died by the hand of the LORD in the land of Egypt, when we sat by the meat pots and ate bread to the full, for you have brought us out into this wilderness

17. Angel, "Moonlit Leadership."
18. Angel, "Moonlit Leadership, 150.

to kill this whole assembly with hunger'" (Exod. 16:2, 3). Each change in the attitude of the people was the result of a transaction.

Since the Hebrew people were so rebellious against Moses, it is interesting to note that they remained loyal to God and to Joshua throughout his time of leadership. In fact, there is only one sin recorded throughout Joshua's tenure, Achan's plunder from Jericho.[19] While Moses was aloof and separate from the people, Joshua was appealing because he allowed people to see his weaknesses, as he did with the disaster at Ai when he tore his clothes and fell prostrate in front of the altar (Josh 7:6). Joshua was a man of prayer and sought God, but he was also a man of the people who commanded their respect.[20] "He was serving the Lord and the Lord's people, and they followed him because they knew they could trust him. His motives were pure, his life was godly, and his character was above reproach."[21] The absence of complaining against Joshua by the people, as they had done to Moses, may be the result of his impressive battlefield record (Exod. 17:8-14) or his "ability to stand up against popular opinion and show himself to be a person with vision and faith."[22] Therefore, even though Moses and Joshua were both great leaders, Joshua provided the transformational leadership that prepared the people for living in the Promised Land.

In the New Testament, there is a striking difference between the transformational leadership of Jesus and the transactional leadership of the Pharisees. Transformational leaders instill "trust, admiration, loyalty, and respect toward the leader, and they are motivated to do more than they originally expected to do."[23] The leadership of Jesus transformed the world by transforming the people he led. This is evident in both his teaching and his actions,

---

19. Angel, "Moonlit Leadership."

20. Wiersbe, *Bible Exposition Commentary*.

21. Wiersbe, *Bible Exposition Commentary*.

22. Fountain, "An Investigation into Successful Leadership Transitions in the Old Testament," 191.

23. Yukl, *Leadership in Organizations*.

often by teaching and modeling the transformational concept of servant leadership.

A central theme in the teachings of Jesus was humility and service. Early in his ministry, he begins the Sermon on the Mount by turning conventional wisdom upside down by saying that the people who are poor in spirit, merciful, and meek are the ones who are blessed (Matt. 5:3-10). He then contrasts the Old Testament law to a revolutionary way of thinking:

> You have heard that it was said to the people long ago, 'You shall not murder, and anyone who murders will be subject to judgment.' But I tell you that anyone who is angry with a brother or sister will be subject to judgment. . . . "You have heard that it was said, 'You shall not commit adultery.' But I tell you that anyone who looks at a woman lustfully has already committed adultery with her in his heart (Matt. 5:21-22, 27-28).

Jesus told a parable about picking seats of honor at a banquet and then concluded by saying "For everyone who exalts himself will be humbled, and he who humbles himself will be exalted" (Luke 14:11, NIV). When the apostles were arguing about who would be the greatest in the kingdom,

> Jesus called them together and said, "You know that the rulers of the Gentiles lord it over them, and their high officials exercise authority over them. Not so with you. Instead, whoever wants to become great among you must be your servant, and whoever wants to be first must be your slave— just as the Son of Man did not come to be served, but to serve, and to give his life as a ransom for many" (Matt. 20:26-28).

Jesus exhibited transformational leadership by challenging his followers to pursue the vision of a pure heart that will naturally result in holy living.

Transformational Leaders in Church History

Throughout history, Christian leaders have followed the examples of scripture and forefathers to transform lives and transform the world. Christian transformational leaders "experienced cognitive dissonance because of their spiritual formation and conditions that they perceived in the environment, and they formed a higher purpose aimed at reducing the dissonance."[24] Martin Luther could no longer accept the corruption and teaching of the Catholic Church, which led him to post the Ninety-Five Theses to the Castle Church in Wittenberg and begin a reformation of the church that transformed lives and led to the emergence of other great church leaders such as Calvin, Zwingli, Wycliffe, and Knox.[25] Alexander Campbell decried Christian sectarianism on the American frontier as *the offspring of hell* and transformed the frontier in the early 19th century with the Restoration Movement.[26] As a school teacher in Calcutta, Mother Teresa became disturbed by the plight of the poor of that city and started a ministry that included 610 missions in 123 countries at the time of her death.[27] Martin Luther King, Jr. was a young Baptist pastor when he decided to act against racial injustice and became the leader of a movement that transformed the attitude of the American culture.[28] Billy Graham became *America's Pastor,* leading 3 million people to Christ, by understanding that "ministry rests on the notion that if individuals are brought to God and their lives transformed, they in turn will go out and transform society."[29] These men and women were transformational leaders who had a significant impact on their world.

David Livingstone became internationally known for his exploration and missionary work in Africa in the 19th century.

24. Jacobs and Longbotham, "The Impact of Spirituality on the Formation of a Leader's Purpose," 69.

25. Booth, *Inspiring Men of Faith.*

26. Foster et al., *The Encyclopedia of the Stone-Campbell Movement.*

27. Kolodiejchuk, *Mother Teresa: Come Be My Light.*

28. Jackson, *From Civil Rights to Human Rights. Martin Luther King Jr. and the Struggle for Economic Justice.*

29. Gibbs and Ostling, "God's Bully Pulpit."

The mind of this transformational Christian leader can begin to be understood by a comment he made to H.M. Stanley, the *New York Herald* reporter who found Livingstone in Africa: "I feel sometimes as if I am only the first evangelist to attack central Africa, crying in the wilderness, and that other evangelists will shortly follow. And after those, there will come a thousand evangelists."[30] Livingstone travelled throughout central Africa, covering an astounding 40,000 miles,[31] and introduced the gospel to countless people who had never heard it before. When he died, the English government demanded that his body be returned to England. The local tribe finally relented, and two men carried his body for eight months and over 1,000 miles to the port, but not until after they removed his heart and internal organs and buried them near their town. Of the 125 million non-whites who lived in 1990 in the ten modern African countries located where Livingstone worked, 75 million (60%) claimed to be Christians.[32]

A single statement transformed the life of young Dwight L (D.L.) Moody, and he used the motivation to transform Chicago and Great Britain. "The world has yet to see what God will do with a man fully consecrated to Him."[33] Moody became determined to be that man by wholly committing his entire life to God. He was not highly educated and not a polished public speaker, so he began by personal evangelism and working with kids one-on-one. When he heard the great Charles Spurgeon preach, he realized that the strength of his preaching came from the Holy Spirit, not from Spurgeon. Based on the confidence that the Holy Spirit would speak through him also, he began to preach. By the end of his life in 1899, before the days of radio and TV, it is estimated that he had proclaimed the gospel in front of 100,000,000 people.[34] Perhaps

---

30. Booth, *Inspiring Men of Faith*, 187.

31. Booth, *Inspiring Men of Faith*.

32. Booth, *Inspiring Men of Faith*.

33. Booth, *Inspiring Men of Faith*, 237.

34. Whitesell, *Great Personal Workers*.

even more impressively, he had worked personally with 750,000 people, many of whom were youth.[35]

As the great transformational leaders in Christian history are considered, it is interesting to note that individuals who are appointed to formal positions of power are not seen to be transformational leaders as a result of their positions. For example, denominational leaders and Popes are seldom mentioned in literature as examples of transformational leadership. One possible explanation is that they seem distant from their followers, as Moses was.

Implications for Today's Leaders

There are several implications of transformational leadership that today's leaders can learn from the minds of historical Christian and biblical leaders. First, transformational leaders must be authentic.[36] Simply being authentic does not make a leader effective and transformational, but a truly transformational leader must be authentic with his followers. Second, relational authenticity is an important component of transformational leadership.[37] In other words, transformational leaders develop relationships with their followers, so they seem to be approachable and genuine. Third, transformational leaders turn followers into leaders.[38] When great transformational leaders die, their work continues because their followers become the leaders. Finally, transformational leaders rally their followers to a cause that is greater than them.[39] These Christian leaders had a common cause as they pointed their followers to Christ.

35. Whitesell, *Great Personal Workers*.

36. Avolio and Gardner, "Authentic Leadership Development."

37. Spitzmuller, "Do They (All) See My True Self? Leader's Relational Authenticity."

38. Burns, *Leadership*.

39. Patterson, Redmer, and Stone, "Transformational Leaders to Servant Leaders versus Level 4 Leaders to Level 5 Leaders - The Move from Good to Great."

Today's Christian leaders can learn from these examples. The common thread that permeates all these stories is the mind of the transformational leader. The successful leader who will transform lives and transform the world will be authentic, will relate well with followers, will nurture leaders, and will point followers to Christ.

Appendix

Measurement Tools

Level 5 Leadership Scale (L5LS)

On a scale of 1 to 10, to what extent do the following characteristics describe the subject? A 1 indicates that this characteristic does not describe him/her at all, while a 10 indicates that it describes him/her exactly.

Personal Humility

- Humble
- Genuine
- A team player
- Servant attitude
- Doesn't seek the spotlight

Indomitable Will

- Intense resolve
- Dedication to the organization
- A clear catalyst in achieving results
- Strong work ethic
- Self-motivated

An average score of at least 7.5 on BOTH personal humility and indomitable will indicate that the subject is a Level 5 leader.[1]

Essential Behaviors of Servant Leadership (EBSL)

The Essential Behaviors of Servant Leadership (EBSL) was developed by Winston and Fields based on a meta-analysis and validation of servant leadership research. The scores of the items of each leader are averaged to determine a single score for the leader on a scale of one to five. Instead of a single benchmark to define servant leadership, there is simply a continuous scale that is useful for comparison. For example, a score of 3.2 may not tell us much but is useful in making comparisons and correlations with other variables.

The list of the ten essential behaviors of servant leadership are:

- Practices what he or she preaches;
- Serves people without regard to their nationality, gender, or race;
- Sees serving as a mission of responsibility to others;
- Shows genuinely interested in employees as people;
- Understands that serving others is most important;
- Is willing to make sacrifices to help others;
- Seeks to instill trust rather than fear or insecurity;
- Is always honest;
- Is driven by a sense of higher calling; and
- Promotes values that transcend self-interest and material success.

1. Reid, "Development of an Instrument to Measure Level 5 Leadership."

Bibliography

Angel, Hayyim. "Moonlit Leadership: A Midrashic Reading of Joshua's Success." *Jewish Bible Quarterly* 37, no. 3 (2009): 144–52.

Arrington, A.V. "Lead with a Human Focus; for Christ's Sake!" *Leadership Advance Online*, no. XIX (2010).

Augustine. *City of God*. Abridged edition, English, 1958. Garden City, N.Y.: Image, 426AD.

Avolio, B.J, and B.M Bass. *Multifactor Leadership Questionnaire. Manual and Sampler Set*. Third. Redwood City, CA: Mindgarden, 2004.

Avolio, Bruce, and Bernard Bass. "MLQ: Self Evaluation Report." Multifactor leadership questionnaire, 2015. https://www.mindgarden.com/multifactor-leadership-questionnaire/627-mlq-self-report-about-me.html.

Avolio, Bruce J., and William L. Gardner. "Authentic Leadership Development: Getting to the Root of Positive Forms of Leadership." *The Leadership Quarterly*, Authentic Leadership Development, 16, no. 3 (June 1, 2005): 315–38. https://doi.org/10.1016/j.leaqua.2005.03.001.

Banks, George, Kelly Davis McCauley, William Gardner, and Courtney Guler. "A Meta-Analytic Review of Authentic and Transformational Leadership: A Test for Redundancy." *The Leadership Quarterly* 27, no. 4 (2016): 634–52.

Barrett, Colleen. "Treat Your People as Family." In *Servant Leadership in Action. How You Can Achieve Great Relationships and Results.*, 183–88. Oakland, CA: Berrett-Koehler Publishers Inc., 2018.

Bass, Bernard, and Ruth Bass. *The Bass Handbook of Leadership: Theory, Research, and Managerial Applications*. Fourth. Free Press, A division of Simon and Schuster, 2008.

Bass, Bernard M. *Leadership and Performance beyond Expectations*. New York : London: Free Press, 1985.

Bass, Bernard M., and Bruce J. Avolio. "Multifactor Leadership Questionnaire," 2015. https://doi.org/10.1037/t03624-000.

Bass, B.M. "From Transactional to Transformational Leadership: Learning to Share the Vision." *Organizational Dynamics*, 1990, 19–31.

Bibliography

Bennett, T.M. "A Study of the Management Leadership Style Preferred by IT Subordinates" 13, no. 2 (2009).

Blanchard, Ken, and Renee Broadwell, eds. *Servant Leadership in Action. How You Can Achieve Great Relationships and Results.* Oakland, CA: Berrett-Koehler Publishers Inc., 2018.

Blanchard, Ken, and Phil Hodges. *Lead Like Jesus Revisited: Lessons from the Greatest Leadership Role Model of All Time.* Revised ed. edition. Nashville, Tennessee: Thomas Nelson, 2016.

Blanchard, Ken, and Spenser Johnson. *The New One Minute Manager.* 1st edition. London: Harper Collins India, 2016.

Bobb, David J. *Humility: An Unlikely Biography of America's Greatest Virtue.* Nashville: Thomas Nelson, 2013.

Booth, E.P. *Inspiring Men of Faith.* Uhlrichsville, OH: Barbour Publishing Inc., 2008.

Brown, Brene. "In the Service of Others." In *Servant Leadership in Action. How You Can Achieve Great Relationships and Results.*, 71–76. Oakland, CA: Berrett-Koehler Publishers Inc., 2018.

Bryant, Adam. "For This Guru, No Question Is Too Big." *The New York Times*, May 23, 2009, sec. Business. https://www.nytimes.com/2009/05/24/business/24collins.html.

Bryant, Phil, and Steven Brown. "Getting to Know the Elephant: A Call to Advance Servant Leadership through Construct Consensus, Empirical Evidence, and Multilevel Theoretical Development." *Servant Leadership: Theory and Practice*, February 1, 2015, 10–35.

Burns, J.M. *Leadership.* New York: Harper and Row, 1978.

Bush, Michael. "Servant Leaders Create a Great Place to Work." In *Servant Leadership in Action. How You Can Achieve Great Relationships and Results.*, 44–49. Oakland, CA: Berrett-Koehler Publishers Inc., 2018.

Catalyst. *Andy Stanley and Jim Collins.* Atlanta, GA, 2008. https://www.youtube.com/watch?v=qZybQo7daVo&t=278s&ab_channel=CatalystLeader.

Collins, Jim. "Concepts - Level 5 Leadership." Jim Collins, 2021. https://www.jimcollins.com/concepts/level-five-leadership.html.

———. "From Good to Great: What Defines a Level V Leader?," 2009. https://www.youtube.com/watch?v=q-KyQ9oXByY&t=1s.

———. *Good to Great. Why Some Companies Make the Leap and Others Don't.* Harper Business, 2001.

———. "The Triumph of Humility and Fierce Resolve." *Harvard Business Review*, 2001, 11.

———. "Where Are You on Your Journey from Good to Great? Good to Great Diagnostic Tool." Boulder, CO, 2006. https://www.jimcollins.com/tools/diagnostic-tool.pdf.

Collins, Jim, and Morten T. Hansen. *Great by Choice: Uncertainty, Chaos, and Luck--Why Some Thrive Despite Them All.* Illustrated edition. New York, NY: Harper Business, 2011.

Bibliography

Collins, Jim, and William Lazier. *BE 2.0 (Beyond Entrepreneurship 2.0): Turning Your Business into an Enduring Great Company*. Portfolio, 2020.

Collins, Jim, and Jerry I. Porras. *Built to Last: Successful Habits of Visionary Companies*. 3rd ed. edition. New York, NY: Harper Business, 1994.

Coudriet, Carter. "Forbes' 2019 College Financial Health Grades: How Fit Is Your School?" Forbes. Accessed January 8, 2021. https://www.forbes.com/sites/cartercoudriet/2019/11/27/how-fit-is-your-school-the-methodology-behind-forbes-2019-college-financial-health-grades/.

Dennis, Robert, and Mihai Bocarnea. "Servant Leadership Assessment Instrument." *Leadership & Organization Development Journal* 26 (December 1, 2005): 600–615. https://doi.org/10.1108/01437730510633692.

Dierendonck, Dirk van. "Servant Leadership: A Review and Synthesis." *Journal of Management* 37, no. 4 (July 1, 2011): 1228–61. https://doi.org/10.1177/0149206310380462.

Drury, Sharon. "Employee Perceptions of Servant Leadership: Comparisons by Level with Job Satisfaction and Organizational Commitment." Dissertation, Regent University, 2004. https://olagroup.com/Images/mmDocument/Drury%20Dissertation%20Spring%2004.pdf.

Duckworth, Angela. *Grit: The Power of Passion and Perseverance*. Illustrated edition. New York: Scribner, 2018.

Erkal, Nisvan, Lata Gangadharan, and Boon Han Koh. "By Chance or By Choice? Biased Attribution of Others' Outcomes." SSRN Scholarly Paper. Rochester, NY: Social Science Research Network, February 29, 2020. https://doi.org/10.2139/ssrn.3251105.

Eva, Nathan, Sen Sendjaya, Daniel Prajogo, Andrew Cavanagh, and Mulyadi Robin. "Creating Strategic Fit: Aligning Servant Leadership with Organizational Structure and Strategy." *Personnel Review* 47, no. 1 (January 1, 2018): 166–86. https://doi.org/10.1108/PR-03-2016-0064.

Focht, A, and M Ponton. "Identifying Primary Characteristics of Servant Leadership: Delphi Study." *International Journal of Leadership Studies* 9, no. 1 (Spring 2015): 44–61.

Foster, D.A., P.M. Blowers, A.L. Dunnavant, and D.N. Williams, eds. *The Encyclopedia of the Stone-Campbell Movement*. Cambridge: Wm. B. Eerdmans Publishing Co., 2004.

Fountain, A. Kay. "An Investigation into Successful Leadership Transitions in the Old Testament." *Asian Journal of Pentecostal Studies* 7, no. 2 (2004): 187–204.

Gibbs, N., and R.N. Ostling. "God's Bully Pulpit." *Time*, November 15, 1993.

Glover, Paul, Paul Glover, and Paul Glover. "The Power of Partners." *Fast Company*, December 22, 2019. https://www.fastcompany.com/1493831/power-partners.

Goleman, Daniel. *Emotional Intelligence: Why It Can Matter More than IQ*. 10th Anniversary edition. New York: Bantam, 2005.

———. "Leadership That Gets Results." *Harvard Business Review*, March 1, 2000. https://hbr.org/2000/03/leadership-that-gets-results.

Bibliography

————. "What Makes a Leader? IQ And Technical Skills Are Important, but Emotional Intelligence Is the Sine qua Non of Leadership." *Harvard Business Review*, December 1998, 93–102.

Greenleaf, Robert K. *Servant Leadership: A Journey into the Nature of Legitimate Power and Greatness.* New York: Paulist Press, 1977.

————. "The Servant as Leader (an Essay)." Greenleaf Organization, 1970. https://archives.yale.edu/repositories/4/resources/10825.

Hansen, Morten. "The 'Man on the Moon' Standard." *Harvard Business Review*, May 25, 2011. https://hbr.org/2011/05/the-man-on-the-moon-standard.

Hogue, Mary. "Gender Bias in Communal Leadership: Examining Servant Leadership." *Journal of Managerial Psychology* 31, no. 4 (January 1, 2016): 837–49. https://doi.org/10.1108/JMP-10-2014-0292.

Howell, J.M., and B.J. Avolio. "Transformational Leadership, Transactional Leadership, Locus of Control, and Support for Innovation: Key Predictors of Consolidated-Business-Unit Performance." *Journal of Applied Psychology* 78, no. 6 (1993): 891–902.

Jackson, T.F. *From Civil Rights to Human Rights. Martin Luther King Jr. and the Struggle for Economic Justice.* Philadelphia, PA: University of Pennsylvania Press, 2007.

Jacobs, G.A., and G.J. Longbotham. "The Impact of Spirituality on the Formation of a Leader's Purpose." *Journal of Management, Spirituality, & Religion* 8, no. 1 (n.d.): 69–91.

Johnson, Ashley. "Johnson: A History." 125 Years of History. Accessed January 8, 2021. https://history.johnsonu.edu/.

Kalina, Peter. "False Humility: The Plague of Genuine Leadership." *International Journal of Business Marketing and Management* 5, no. 8 (2020): 4.

Khan, Muhammad Mumtaz, Muhammad Shujaat Mubarik, and Tahir Islam. "Leading the Innovation: Role of Trust and Job Crafting as Sequential Mediators Relating Servant Leadership and Innovative Work Behavior." *European Journal of Innovation Management*, 2020. https://doi.org/10.1108/EJIM-05-2020-0187.

Kiker, D. Scott, Judith Scully Callahan, and Mary Brlek Kiker. "Exploring the Boundaries of Servant Leadership: A Meta-Analysis of the Main and Moderating Effects of Servant Leadership on Behavioral and Affective Outcomes." *Journal of Managerial Issues* 31, no. 2 (2019): 172–97.

Kolodiejchuk, B. *Mother Teresa: Come Be My Light.* New York: Doubleday Religion, 2007.

Kouzes, James M., and Barry Z. Posner. "Finding Your Voice." In *Servant Leadership in Action. How You Can Achieve Great Relationships and Results.*, 109–14. Oakland, CA: Berrett-Koehler Publishers Inc., 2018.

Kruse, Kevin. "100 Best Quotes on Leadership." *Forbes*, October 16, 2012. https://www.forbes.com/sites/kevinkruse/2012/10/16/quotes-on-leadership/.

Lee, Ye Hoon. "Emotional Intelligence, Servant Leadership, and Development Goal Orientation in Athletic Directors." *Sport Management Review* 22, no. 3 (June 1, 2019): 395–406. https://doi.org/10.1016/j.smr.2018.05.003.

Lehrke, Alyse Scicluna, and Kristin Sowden. "Servant Leadership and Gender." In *Servant Leadership and Followership: Examining the Impact on Workplace Behavior*, edited by Crystal J. Davis. Cham: Springer International Publishing, 2017. https://doi.org/10.1007/978-3-319-59366-1.

Leighton, Mara. "The 31 Most Influential Books Ever Written about Business." Business Insider, 2019. https://www.businessinsider.com/influential-business-books.

Lemoine, G. James, and Terry C. Blum. "Servant Leadership, Leader Gender, and Team Gender Role: Testing a Female Advantage in a Cascading Model of Performance." *Personnel Psychology* 74, no. 1 (2021): 3–28. https://doi.org/10.1111/peps.12379.

Lencioni, Patrick M. *The Ideal Team Player: How to Recognize and Cultivate the Three Essential Virtues.* 1st edition. Hoboken, New Jersey: Jossey-Bass, 2016.

Lewis, C. S. *Mere Christianity.* Revised&Enlarged edition. San Francisco: HarperOne, 2015.

Lewis, C.S. *The Screwtape Letters.* New York: The Macmillan Company, 1943. https://www.goodreads.com/work/best_book/2920952-the-screwtape-letters.

Lichtenwalner, Ben. "Servant Leadership Lesson: Jim Collins at Chick-Fil-A Leadercast." *Modern Servant Leader* (blog), May 24, 2010. https://www.modernservantleader.com/servant-leadership/servant-leadership-lesson-jim-collins-at-chick-fil-a-leadercast/.

Maney, Kevin. "True Believers Ignite Super Sales Rate for 'Good to Great.'" *USA Today*, May 18, 2004. https://usatoday30.usatoday.com/money/books/2004-05-18-good-to-great_x.htm.

Mark, J.J. "Nebuchadnezzar II." *World History Encyclopedia*, 2018. https://www.worldhistory.org/Nebuchadnezzar_II/.

Maslow, Abraham. *The Farther Reaches of Human Nature.* New York: Viking, 1971.

May, Rob. "'Good to Great' Review: Why 'Good to Great' Isn't Very Good." Business Pundit, 2006. https://www.businesspundit.com/why-good-to-great-isnt-very-good/.

Merriam-Webster. "Dictionary by Merriam-Webster," 2020. https://www.merriam-webster.com/.

Moreno, J. Edward. "Obama: Trump 'Takes Responsibility for Nothing but Takes Credit for Everything.'" Text. TheHill, August 14, 2020. https://thehill.com/homenews/campaign/512035-obama-trump-takes-responsibility-for-nothing-but-takes-credit-for.

Morris, J. Andrew, Céleste M. Brotheridge, and John C. Urbanski. "Bringing Humility to Leadership: Antecedents and Consequences of Leader

Bibliography

Humility." *Human Relations* 58, no. 10 (2005): 1323–50. https://doi. org/10.1177/0018726705059929.

Muller, R, and J.R Turner. "Matching the Project Manager's Leadership Style to Project Type." *International Journal of Project Management* 25 (2007): 21–32.

Nordbye, Valorie C, and Justin A Irving. "Servant Leadership and Organizational Effectiveness: Examining Leadership Culture among Millennials within a US National Campus Ministry." *Servant Leadership* 4, no. 1 (2017): 22.

Northouse, Peter G. *Leadership: Theory and Practice.* Eighth edition. Los Angeles: SAGE Publications, Inc, 2019.

Lexico Dictionaries | English. "Oxford Dictionary on Lexico.Com," 2020. https://www.lexico.com/.

Parris, Denise Linda, and Jon Welty Peachey. "A Systematic Literature Review of Servant Leadership Theory in Organizational Contexts." *Journal of Business Ethics* 113, no. 3 (2013): 377–93. https://doi.org/10.1007/s10551-012-1322-6.

Patterson, Kathleen, Timothy Redmer, and Gregory Stone. "Transformational Leaders to Servant Leaders versus Level 4 Leaders to Level 5 Leaders - The Move from Good to Great." Virginia Beach, VA, 2003. https://studylib.net/ doc/8660025/transformational-leaders-to-servant-leaders-versus-level-4.

Penn Wharton School. "Good Vs. Great Leaders: The Difference Is Humility, Doubt and Drive." Knowledge@Wharton, June 20, 2001. https:// knowledge.wharton.upenn.edu/article/good-vs-great-leaders-the-difference-is-humility-doubt-and-drive/.

Phillips, Amber. "Analysis | Everyone and Everything Trump Has Blamed for His Coronavirus Response." *Washington Post.* Accessed December 21, 2020. https://www.washingtonpost.com/politics/2020/03/31/everyone-everything-trump-has-blamed-his-coronavirus-response/.

Radu, Cătălina, Alecxandrina Deaconu, and Corina Frăsineanu. "Leadership and Gender Differences—Are Men and Women Leading in the Same Way?" *Contemporary Leadership Challenges*, February 1, 2017. https://doi. org/10.5772/65774.

Ramsey, David. "Leading Is Serving." In *Servant Leadership in Action. How You Can Achieve Great Relationships and Results.*, 44–49. Oakland, CA: Berrett-Koehler Publishers Inc., 2018.

Reid, Wilbur. "A Sabbatical for Volunteers." *Christian Standard*, January 17, 2010, 47–48.

———. "Development of an Instrument to Measure Level 5 Leadership." Ph.D., Regent University, 2012. https://search.proquest.com/ docview/1420266122/abstract/60B97851677E4035PQ/1.

———. "Service & Humility in Crisis Leadership: Intriguing Theories, but Do They Actually Produce Results?" Brussels, Belgium, 2017. https:// www.scribd.com/document/487090594/Service-and-Humility-in-Crisis-Leadership-Intriguing-Theories-But-Do-They-Actually-Produce-Results.

Bibliography

———. *Service & Humility in Crisis Leadership: Intriguing Theories, but Do They Actually Produce Results?*, 2020. https://www.youtube.com/watch?v=3w8t7V_Ljp4&ab_channel=WilburReid.

———. "Service and Humility in Leadership: Intriguing Theories, but Do They Actually Produce Results?" Atlanta, GA, 2016. https://convention2.allacademic.com/one/ila/ila16/index.php?cmd=Online+Program+Download+Document&document_type=document&key=online_program_view_paper_downloads&document_key=82a4554ab2ced11ed1cb7d0590 5b6f4c&filename=ila16_proceeding_1135778.pdf&PHPSESSID=vamrm p2uomh2e854t12j5a6ruj.

———. "Service and Humility in Leadership: Intriguing Theories, but Do They Actually Produce Results?" *Servant Leadership: Theory and Practice* 4, no. 2 (2017): 27–52.

———. "The Impact of Religious Commitment on Servant and Level 5 Leadership," 2020. https://www.scribd.com/document/487175496/Servant-and-Level -5-Leadership-and-Religion.

———. "The Mind of the Transformational Leader." In *True Leadership: Leadership Styles and the Kenotic Relationship*, 1st ed. 2020 edition. Palgrave Macmillan, 2020.

———. *Zervant Leadership - Because Servant Leadership Is Not Enough*, 2018. https://www.youtube.com/watch?v=c00SOXH92fk&feature=youtu.be.

Rezvani, Azadeh, Rowena Barrett, and Pouria Khosravi. "Investigating the Relationships among Team Emotional Intelligence, Trust, Conflict and Team Performance." *Team Performance Management: An International Journal* 25, no. 1/2 (January 1, 2019): 120–37. https://doi.org/10.1108/ TPM-03-2018-0019.

Robinson, Anthony. "Leadership That Matters: Lessons from and for the Parish." *The Christian Century*, December 15, 1999. https://www.christiancentury. org/article/2011-07/leadership-matters.

Serfontein, Kobus, and Johan Hough. "Nature of the Relationship between Strategic Leadership, Operational Strategy and Organisational Performance." *South African Journal of Economic and Management Sciences* 14, no. 4 (January 2011): 393–406.

Sims, Ronald R. *Managing Organizational Behavior*. Greenwood Publishing Group, 2002.

Sisodia, Raj. "Servant Leadership Is Conscious Leadership." In *Servant Leadership in Action. How You Can Achieve Great Relationships and Results.*, 19–25. Oakland, CA: Berrett-Koehler Publishers Inc., 2018.

Sisodia, Rajendra S. "Understanding the Performance Drivers of Conscious Firms." *California Management Review* 55, no. 3 (May 1, 2013): 87–96. https://doi.org/10.1525/cmr.2013.55.3.87.

Slvanathan, N, and G.C Fekken. "Emotional Intelligence, Moral Reasoning, and Transformational Leadership." *Leadership and Organizational Development Journal* 23, no. 4 (2002): 198–204.

Bibliography

Spector, Robert. *Shared Values: A History of Kimberly-Clark*. 1St Edition. Lyme, CT: Greenwich Pub. Group, 1997.

Spitzmuller, M. "Do They (All) See My True Self? Leader's Relational Authenticity." *European Journal of Work and Organizational Psychology* 19, no. 3 (2010): 304–32.

Stone, A.G., R.F. Russell, and K. Patterson. "Transformational versus Servant Leadership: A Difference in Leader Focus." *The Leadership and Organization Development Journal25* 25, no. 4 (2004): 349–61.

The Holy Bible: New International Version, Containing the Old Testament and the New Testament. Grand Rapids, MI: Zondervan Bible Publishers, 1978.

Tzu, Lao. *The Complete Works of Lao Tzu: Tao Teh Ching and Hua Hu Ching*. Translated by Hua-Ching Ni. SevenStar Communications, 2013.

Virtuous Leadership. "Darwin Smith," September 14, 2016. https://hvli.org/models/darwin-smith/.

Warren, Rick. *The Purpose Driven Life*. 1st edition. Grand Rapids, Mich: Zondervan, 2002.

Washington Post. *Trump Will Claim Credit for (Almost) Anything*, 2019. https://www.youtube.com/watch?v=VMoGFk3vi54&ab_channel=WashingtonPost.

Whitesell, Faris Daniel. *Great Personal Workers*. Moody Press, 1956.

Wiersbe, W.W. *Bible Exposition Commentary: Old Testament Wisdom and Poetry*. New York: Victor, 1989.

Royal Scribe. "Wilbur, Linda Reid Second Mile Award Honors Lifestyle of Service," March 31, 2017. https://royalscribe.net/2017/03/31/wilbur-linda-reid-second-mile-award-honors-lifestyle-of-service/.

Winston, B, and D Fields. "Seeking and Measuring the Essential Behaviors of Servant Leadership." *Leadership and Organization Development Journal* 36, no. 4 (2015): 413–34.

Wong, Paul, and Dean Davey. "Best Practices in Servant Leadership." Virginia Beach, VA: Regent University, 2007. http://www.drpaulwong.com/wp-content/uploads/2013/09/wong-davey-2007-best-practices-in-servant-leadership.pdf.

Wright, N. T., Dale Larsen, and Sandy Larsen. *Colossians and Philemon*. Downers Grove, Ill: IVP Connect, 2009.

Yammarino, F.J., W.D. Spangler, and B.M. Bass. "Transformational Leadership and Performance: A Longitudinal Investigation." *The Leadership Quarterly* 4, no. 1 (1993): 81–102.

Yukl, G. *Leadership in Organizations*. Upper Saddle River, NJ: Pearson Prentice Hall, 2006.